Sahil Sood was born in Ludhiana, Punjab, India. He is a Chartered Accountant by profession. He discovered his love of reading and writing at a young age, getting published in academic journals and newspapers. "A Thousand Dreams Within Me Softly Burn" is his debut novel. He can be reached at sahilsood042@gmail.com.

A Thousand Dreams Within Me Softly Burn

Sahil Sood

Published by Woven Words Publishers OPC Pvt. Ltd., 2016
Copyright© Sahil Sood, 2016

Sahil Sood has asserted his right under the Indian Copyrights Act 1957 to be identified as the author of this work.

This book is sold to the condition that it shall not, by way of trade or otherwise, be lent, resold, hired out, or otherwise circulated without the publisher's prior consent in any form of binding or cover other than that in which it is published and without a similar condition, including this condition, being imposed on the subsequent purchaser.

ISBN-13: **978-1541165021**
ISBN-10: **1541165020**
Price: **$10**

This book is a work of fiction. All names, characters, places, addresses and incidents are fictitious and product of the author's imagination. Any resemblance with any events, locales, persons-living or dead, is purely coincidental.

Woven Words Publishers OPC Pvt. Ltd.,
Vill: Raipur, P.O: Raipur Paschimbar, Dist: Purba Midnapore, Pin: 721401, West Bengal, India.
www.wovenwordspublishers.com

ACKNOWLEDGEMENTS

This book would not have been possible without the guidance of *Arnold Weinstein* from Brown University, USA, whose online course "The Fiction of Relationship" helped me mature as a discerning, emotional reader. I owe a great debt to his online lectures and suggested reading list, which transformed the process of reading and writing for me.

I would like to thank my friends—Roopali Chaturvedi and Jaspreet Chera, for their unstinting help and exacting critique to help me fine-tune the manuscript. My first readers—Nimisha Uniyal, Ashween Dara, John Rathee, and Stuti Sharma, for their perceptive feedback. My close friends—Radhika Sharma, Sakshi Arora, Apurva Katyal, and Arsh Behal, for their love and encouragement.

I owe gratitude to my family—my mother, Shamina Sood; my father, Rakesh Sood; and my sister, Arshia Sood, for investing their faith in me and standing like strong pillars of support behind me every time. My grandparents—Ramesh Chand Sood, Raj Kumar Sood, Late Sudesh Sood, and Late Usha Sood, for their unconditional love. Asad Dhaumya, for helping me discover this beautiful title from *Arthur Rimbaud's* "Evening Prayer". My extended family—Shaminder Sood, Madhulika Sood, Madhurima Gangwar, Abhimanyu Sood, Gaurav Dhanda, and Shiven Sood, for giving me a lifetime of beautiful memories. My language teachers at school—Mala Choudhary, Gurmeet Kaur, Inderpreet Parihar, Neera Puri, and Neelam Kaushal, for introducing me to the subtle joys of reading literature and helping me shape my creative vision.

I would like to express gratitude to my publisher, Woven Words Publishers, for taking this journey with me. And lastly to my friends, Gagan and Anandi, for all the journeys that never reached their desired destination.

In loving memory of Late Usha Sood

For bringing the gift of music in our lives...

"Maybe there is nothing, ever, that can equal the recollection of having been young together."
– Michael Cunningham, The Hours

"I'm still there, watching those possessed children, as far away from the mystery now as I was then. I've never written, though I thought I wrote, never loved, though I thought I loved, never done anything but wait outside the closed door."
– Marguerite Duras, The Lover

"...this was not as real as my despairing sense that nothing was real for me, nothing would ever be real for me again – unless, indeed, this sensation of falling was reality..."
– James Baldwin, Giovanni's Room

"A thousand Dreams within me softly burn: From time to time my heart is like some oak whose blood runs golden where a branch is torn."

– Arthur Rimbaud, **Evening Prayer**

Dear Siddharth,

I am barely able to contain my excitement at having found you, at last! Before I begin, let me tell you that I have been looking for you for the last ten years.

I was twelve when I first watched Rajinder Singh Bedi's 'Dastak (The Knock)' on cable television. I have watched it multiple times since then. Growing up next to a ghetto in a crowded city like New Delhi, I was quite aware of the struggles of everyday life of middle-class people such as myself. We lived in a rented single-room accommodation. My father was away for most of the time. There were constant squabbles and fights in our neighborhood. The voices would ring ceaselessly from morning till night—shrill, angry, drunken, and miserable.

My mother and I always kept the main door and windows locked. Men would try to peep in occasionally and pass lewd comments. My mother always shielded me from the shame. She wanted me to get a good education and shift to a decent neighborhood once I started earning. This was her only hope.

We worshipped cinema and music. Though we could never afford to watch movies in a theatre, my mother made earnest requests to our cable operator to play the old classics from the sixties and seventies. She ensured that I watched all the films that she had grown up watching and cherishing.

There is a song in 'Dastak', sung by Lata Mangeshkar, called 'Baiyan Naa Dharo Balma'. Just before the song begins there is a faint music in the background: another version of the same song in Thumri, sung by Shobha Gurtu. I know this now because I spent days and night searching the name of the singer. I had never heard such a sublime melody in my life. Her voice sounded immaculate—full of passion, yearning, and desire.

During my high school years, I happened to chance upon an essay titled 'The Lost Thumris of Cinema', in some archives on the Internet. I remember being highly impressed by the research, but more than that it was the candid, free-style approach that piqued my curiosity to know the name of the author. Your writing has been the singular inspiration behind my own writing career. I have re-visited your essay countless times—in doubt, curiosity, frustration, and joy. I discover something new every time.

I have spent years trying to locate you. There is no mention of you anywhere on the Internet. I even visited your hometown. They said you worked briefly at the Indian Express before resigning. Finally, I got your e-mail id from an editor who knew you personally. A lot has happened since then, a lot is still happening on education and career front, mainly. I now live in Mumbai with my parents. I even got my mother a bunch of DVDs of all her favorite films, from my savings. At first, she chided me for being reckless with money, but of late she has warmed down. I know she appreciates the gesture deeply.

Before I go further, I want to confess something: I think I'm becoming drawn to you. I always have; in fact, right from the moment I read the first sentence of your essay till typing this letter to you.

I am twenty-two years old now and have never been romantically involved with anyone in my life. Your words fill the void of romance in my life. There is an undercurrent of strange yearning and at the same time deep fulfillment in them. This feeling is new to me. I've never in my entire limited life span come across a person as mature, bold, extremely sensitive and sharp as you, and also who shares a passionate liking for reading, music, and cinema.

The reason why I feel compelled to write to you is because I feel at my age, or any age for that matter, one should express what one feels intensely—it's one of the few joys of living and what makes one human.

I have no clue of what you do professionally, where you live, or what your likes/dislikes are. I hope you're still writing. There is no rational explanation for what I've been feeling for the last several years, and therefore, you will probably be a little hassled to reply with politeness and tact.

I had resisted writing this for a long time. You are everything I look for in the person of my dreams. I hope this doesn't worry, annoy, or outrage you.

Warmly,
Gautam

Saaransh

Siddharth was awakened by a gentle knock at the door. He checked his alarm; it was six in the morning. He got up from the bed feeling groggy and lightheaded. He put on his spectacles and staggered towards the door. He squinted through the curtains and saw Mariam, the owner of the guesthouse, waiting outside.

"Sorry to disturb, professor, but a female friend of yours has been calling since last night. Your phone is switched off. She says it's urgent. She has asked you to call her on this number as soon as you can," she said, handing over a slip of paper to Siddharth.

"I will. Sorry for your trouble. I had a severe headache last night. The medicine makes me drowsy," he replied politely, taking the slip from her hand. Mariam departed with a sympathetic smile.

The morning was crisp and bright. There was a tranquil hush in the air. The mountains appeared tall and majestic in the early rays of the sun. A plume of white smoke skimmed comfortably over the lower slopes.

Siddharth ambled along the corridor for some time. He noticed that the floor was still wet with precipitation from last night. The sky looked ashen blue with a potent yellow slowly spreading over its surface.

The courtyard was bathed in weak sunlight. A host of sparrows crowded around the small earthen dish bowls that Mariam filled every morning. They pecked and chirped innocently. Siddharth waved to the fellow travellers who had woken early and were ready to leave for their journey. He slowly walked back to his room and dialed the number on the slip.

"Hi, Siddharth here. May I know who this is?" he asked.

"Siddharth! It's Radhika! Why is your phone switched off?" Radhika answered.

"Radhika! Hi! I am really sorry. It was raining last night and I was feeling a little under the weather. I had switched it off so that I could have a decent sleep. Anyway, what's the urgency?"

"Your article got published yesterday."

"Really? But you had asked me to make the paragraph transitions smoother. I was still working on that," he expressed in a confused tone.

"The Board decided to go ahead and publish it anyway. I protested. I told them you were still fixing the structure. Apparently, they liked it so much that they were unwilling to make any changes in it."

"That's strange. And what about the title?"

"That's the reason I have been calling you. None of us could understand why you would title it such. We wanted to ask you for an alternative title."

"And? What did you finally do?"

"We went ahead and published it as such. We really struggled to change it, but then gave up thinking it might have a special significance in your life."

"How thoughtful! You're the best editor anyone could ask for!"

"Yeah, but you still have to tell me why this title? It sounds...strange."

"I will explain some other time. I promise. Now, tell me where I can read it. I have spent months researching the content. I can't believe it's finally out there!"

"Just log on to our portal and click on the *Arts & Culture* tab. The first article is yours."

"Thank you so much! I will check it in some time. How have you been, otherwise?"

"I am fine. The workplace is same—frantic, yet dull."

"Have you considered looking for a different organization?"

"No. I am going to give it another two years. Kush and I are planning to have our first child."

"That's great! It's a big decision. I hope you're planning wisely."

"We have been discussing it for some time. The timing seems ideal. Kush and I have well-paying jobs now. There are no mortgages on the house. Also, mom has moved in with us. So, it will be a great help once the baby is here and we are out, working."

"That seems settled then. I am really happy for you guys! Come and visit me in Shimla sometime. The school guesthouse is quite comfortable. We don't get many visitors in the village."

"We will plan something. When are you leaving from Manali?"

"Tomorrow. The school re-opens on Monday, though. I am planning to get back early."

"Are you ever coming back?"

"Where?"

"Chandigarh."

A brief silence ensued. "I don't know. I like working at the school. The children love me. I don't see a life back in Chandigarh."

"You have been gone for years now. The last I heard your parents moved back to New Delhi. I was going through your article and it seemed like you had done a lot of research on it. It is strange...living in obscurity when you could be so famous. You have a rare talent, Siddharth. I hope you know that. You just need a little finesse—and right platform."

"Radhika, I don't want to go over this again. This is my life now. I love my school, my books, my children, and my space. I write whenever I can. It keeps me busy—besides, I am trying to get back to writing. I know I am a little rusty.

It has been years since I got published. I hope to change that soon."

"It is fine then, I guess," she sighed with resignation. "Go on to the portal and read your article. We are getting a good response."

Siddharth opened his laptop and quickly browsed through the tabs. He found his article featured on the top ten most read articles since yesterday.

Saaransh: A Voyage Through Literature and Cinema
Monday, 27ᵗʰ June 2016
By Siddharth Kapoor

Figure 1: The Lighthouse, National Museum of Scotland

Are we going to the lighthouse tomorrow? No. Yes. Perhaps. I don't know.

The wistful and elegiac quality of this sentence from **Virginia Woolf's 'To the Lighthouse'** can be compared to a shaft of light breaking from a thin crevice: growing wider and wider; losing themselves in the soft advancing light, the weary souls heave a sigh of relief; a momentary blip in time, return of the lost spring they hail, until the light starts fading away, dying, leaving them groping in darkness; the light fades away faster and faster, hitting back at the hard surface, dissolving into what **Virginia Woolf** famously describes as *"the wedge-shaped core of darkness."*

Perhaps. I don't know. Can despondency wear one out? Will we ever go to the lighthouse? Thus, begins **Woolf's** timeless inquiry into human longing and search for identity.

"But what have I done with my life? Thought Mrs. Ramsay, taking her place at the head of the table, and looking at all the plates making white circles on it. "William, sit by me," she said. "Lily," she said, wearily, "over there." They had that – Paul Rayley and Minta Doyle – she, only this – an infinitely long table and plates and knives. At the far end was her husband, sitting down, all in a heap, frowning. What at? She did not know. She did not mind. She could not understand how she had ever felt any emotion or affection for him. She had a sense of being past everything, through everything, out of everything, ..."

In the above paragraph from **Woolf's 'To the Lighthouse'**, we see Mrs. Ramsay, a middle-aged housewife, sitting at one end of a long table at dinner time, brooding over the daunting, timeless query: Who am I? The book paints a portrait of a lady who is trapped in the chains of domestic life, the same chains that bind and confine her to becoming the 'be-all' and 'end-all' of her family. Thus, Mrs. Ramsay helps us understand that we may not even own ourselves and that family may be a cocoon where the self lives and where it might die.

Which brings us to the question: Do we know ourselves? Perhaps it would be safe to say that we discover ourselves along the way. Perhaps it is the remarkable accidents of chance, fate, and encounter that determine who we are.

And when, if ever, do we stop becoming? Even our death may not finalize these things. Look at a figure like Richard

Nixon, one of the most chameleonic figures in American politics—the number of turns of the forking path of Nixon's career, including that last stint as an elder statesman, after earlier episodes of disgrace and humiliation.

What about writers like **Herman Melville** who lived out the dead letter curse in the story **'Bartleby'**, and who himself was a disappeared, invisible man, for most of his life after the eighteen fifties? He lived decades and decades after that. But no one talked about him. People didn't read him. People didn't think he was an important writer. Look now at what we think. He is not alive to tell us how much he enjoys it, but certainly, if we were to ask what is the identity of **Melville**, we would have to say that it is something that outreaches by far what he could have known. This is true for so many writers. It is true for **Homer**. It is true for **Socrates**. It is true, perhaps, for all of us. Do we really know our end-stage, our definitive identity? It is a forking path line and perhaps eternity is actually the right unit of time and measure to gauge how we continue to evolve and become.

The desire to blend in others is the founding stone of all human gratification.

To continually evolve is to acquire new characteristics that are a mere response to external stimuli. "Law of Metamorphosis" i.e. "to become the other" is **Kafka's law**, and is dramatized in both his classic works—**'Metamorphosis' and 'A Country Doctor'**.

In **'Metamorphosis'** Gregor Samsa suffered a fate that any bug would have, had it been disturbing the peace of everyday lives of its keepers. **Kafka's** work is remorseless. It is an unflinching look at how it might be to exit the human.

In **'A Country Doctor' Kafka** heightens the nauseating effect that might ensue by projecting one's deep-seated fears and injunctions of flesh on another human being. The text has a voyeuristic appeal that not only illuminates the mysteries of duty and sex but also how urgent and insurmountable is our desire to connect, to enmesh with others.

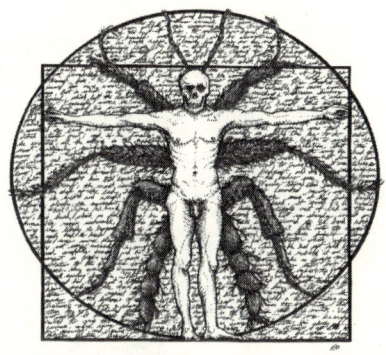

Figure 2: "The Metamorphosis", Landis Blair Illustrations

"To become the other" is perhaps what made a fifty-two-year-old professor, David Lurie, the protagonist of **J.M. Coetzee's 'Disgrace'**, solemnly reconsider his climacteric position upon examining a goat's swollen scrotum. That imprinting of one's own fears and desires on someone's wounds makes one realize of his/her own debilitating circumstances, is a classic example of **Kafka's law.**

In **Ingmar Bergman's 'Persona'**, we see a nurse's and an actress's personalities entangle while they search for identity through memories. It is a classic example of the law of metamorphosis that **Kafka** talks about in his text. The two females in the movie develop a strange communion wherein they imprint their fears and desires on each other, altogether resisting the urge to become the other. Thus, personality is both plural and singular. In his essay on the movie, the famous American movie critic, **Roger Ebert**, wrote: Most of what we think of "ourselves" is not direct experience of the world, but a mental broadcast made of ideas, memories, media input, other people, jobs, roles, duties, lusts, hopes, fears.

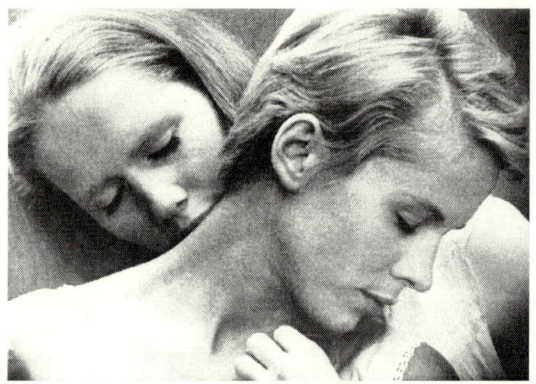

Figure 3: A still from 'Persona'

How much of you is your past?

In **Charlotte Bronte's 'Jane Eyre'**, we read about a young Jane, fist-bound to a chair in a dark gloomy cellar, believed to be housing the spirit of her great uncle. It is when she looks in the mirror, which **Bronte** famously calls as *the visionary hollows*, she sees a long history of abuse and neglect that taints and mars her appearance. This single incident changes the course of her life and by the end of the book we see her emerging as a feisty, self-assertive woman who spurns the tender advances of her tyrannical lover and courses a path of her own will. All through the book we see her struggling under the oppressive regime of class structure, which brings back the wounds of her own oppressive past; and perhaps it was the resolute will of not falling victim to her past that transformed her.

To what extent are we the prisoners of our compulsive desires?

"Sometimes he thought of it in that way, remembering the hard, untearful and unselfpitying and almost manlike yielding of that surrender. A spiritual privacy so long intact that its own instinct for preservation had immolated it, its physical phase the strength and fortitude of a man. A dual personality: the one the woman at first sight of whom in the lifted candle (or perhaps the very sound of the slippered approaching feet) there had opened before him, instantaneous as a landscape in a lightning flash, a horizon of physical security and adultery if not pleasure; the other the mantrained muscles and the mantrained habit of thinking born of heritage and environment with which he had to fight up to the final instant. There was no feminine vacillation, no coyness of obvious desire and intention to succumb at last. It was as if he struggled physically with another man for an object of no actual value to either, and for which they struggled on principle alone."

This beautifully layered text from **William Faulkner's 'Light in August'** heightens the magnitude of sexual desire; repressed anger; clash of masculine and feminine virtues; parental abuse; and irrepressible and seething violence that the narrator is in captivity of. We see him committing heinous acts of violence throughout the book. And we see how racial bigotry plays a key role in fuelling his violent urges and condemning him to a life of oppression, with no scope for redemption. It is a classic example of how our compulsive urges can inhibit and chain us forever.

Abbe Provost's deeply affecting novel, **'Manon Lescaut'**, further problematizes our desire for connection: the sublime unity of both lovers, which is so ardently desired but less likely achieved.

Des Grieux, a seventeen-year-old adolescent boy who is destined for an ecclesiastical career, meets the young and beautiful Manon on his way and experiences a whole new set of sensations that soon override his ambition and act at the helm of all his future life choices. We see him becoming a murderer, a thief, and a scoundrel—his every act of notoriety justified by his desire to maintain his alliance with Manon. Interestingly, he doesn't reproach himself with all his acts that deem strong condemnation but rather accords himself with the highest sense of virtue—the virtue of a tenacious lover whose noble, exultant picture of love is equivalent to religion and who hopes to be bountifully repaid for all the troubles undertaken.

For Manon, love is not enough for sustenance, and she impetuously engages herself in turbulent love affairs with wealthy men. The possibility of maintaining her love for Des Grieux hinges grotesquely on material assets and resources. She even remarks on one occasion that the fidelity she expects of him is that of the heart and not of the body. One would call her bold, rash, ruthless, debauched, materialistic, and indecisive, but what one fails to see is how different her philosophy of love and life is from Des Grieux's.

Would you call them a couple or two separate individuals? Is it true that Des Grieux loves Manon, but doesn't understand her love ethos? Is his love ethos significantly different from Manon's? Do they have to be consistent with hers? We see as the story progresses how money plays a central role in whether or not this couple can maintain their alliance.

We like to flirt with the idea of "two bodies, one soul", but how often does that happen? We say we want the other person to be happy. What we mean is, we want them to be happy with us, just as we are, on our terms. This inconsistency in their perspectives lead the two lovers to their fatal end and establishes **'Manon Lescaut'** as an enduring piece of classic literature whose relevance holds even today, after two hundred years since it was first published.

Figure 4: Manon's Death, Jean Jacques-Pasquier

In **Inaritu's 'Babel'**, we see a group of people from different nationalities and cultures trapped in alien lands where they are befallen by tragic incidents. We see them calling out for help, but to whom? Their cries fall on deaf ears. As per Ebert, "[t]hey desperately want to utter that word or sentence but are prevented because of – the language barrier, their cultural assumptions, and the inability of others to comprehend what they are actually saying [...]"
Here, the language and the cultural constraints lock them out of establishing connectivity.

Now I come to the central question of the whole

discussion: How do literature and cinema help us understand relationships? And while addressing that I would also like to answer: Is connectivity possible?

To the latter, I would respond by alluding to the relationship between Mr. and Mrs. Ramsay in **Virginia Woolf's 'To the Lighthouse'**. In one sequence, we see Mr. Ramsay admiring Mrs. Ramsay's flowers; while as readers we know that for a self-hardened and self-obsessed character it is unlikely of him to obsess and brood over anything but himself and his work. But as readers, we also realize that perhaps the most epic voyage of human life is to exit your own precincts by dent of love into those of another. And maybe it matters less how far you get than you even seek to do it.

Thus, we see the mute Japanese girl, frustrated with her unmet sexual desires, reaching out to the cop in the last shot of **Inaritu's 'Babel'** after being humiliated by him. In a note, the details of which were never shown in the film, it is suggested that she tries to make him understand her grievous circumstances by mentioning the incestuous relationship she shared with her father, and how that lead to her mother committing suicide.

Figure 5: A still from 'Babel'

Reading and viewing are essential because we know that surface notations are the cheat. It is the surface depiction of things what locks us out of the teeming, throbbing, libidinous and emotional world that we inhabit, and that relationship is precisely the arena where all of it comes to the fore.

The human brain is pernicious—it muddles things up. The very project of order that we pride ourselves on is also a way of distorting reality. Reality itself is intermixed, fresh except that ordinarily, we don't have a clue of it. Literature and cinema provide a language for all the bouts of effect, anger and desire that punctuate life and escape our observation most of the times. They remind us of what a spectacle our real world is both inside and outside.

Measures that are appropriate to and through art are radically different from the kind of empirical measures that we can find in the sciences and in the social sciences and in computer science, kinds of things that are measurable. But the measure of the human, the moral, the imaginative, the emotional, the neural, measures, it seems to me, find their privileged site in art. And these literary texts and films describe, make visible to us, and allow us to share stories where we either connect with or collide with each other and our world.

As in life and fiction, we tend to associate ourselves strongly with experiences that help us in establishing our identity. We are enmeshed with others; our feelings and emotions are keyed to others; our very being is a mix of shaping and being shaped. What one experiences during a lifetime, is often hard to define in terms of the impact it creates on oneself. Reading fiction and viewing cinema is not just a stimulative exercise but a voyeuristic journey into one's inner self, experienced through the fate of others, both real and imaginary, compelling one to ask hard questions, letting one meditate on his/her true motivations and deepest fears. Thus, it is the truth within the lie that offers true catharsis. It makes the ambiguities of life seem universal and helps in shaping a global human being that is fed through some sensory nervous passage carrying emotions of love, fear, hatred, resentment, forgiveness, compassion, and wonderment from all over.

Are we going to the lighthouse tomorrow? Yes.

The shaft of light breaking from the thin crevice grows wider and wider until the vision starts clearing and the once weary souls, now in full grip of ecstasy shout with joy!

The *lighthouse* reminds us that all the waters that surround us are traversable. Human memory and human creation through art are inseparable and are faces of each other.

Lovers and Travellers

"Excuse me, sir, do you mind if I take this seat? It is full everywhere else," the stranger asked. Siddharth peered over his spectacles and saw a young boy, possibly in his early twenties, looking at him eagerly. He was carrying a backpack on his shoulders.

"No, please have a seat," Siddharth replied. The boy looked extremely relieved. He grinned at Siddharth and took the seat opposite to him.

"Thank you very much, sir. I have been touring all the cafés here for the past two hours. They are all full. Peak season—they say," he said.

"Yes. The place is thronging with visitors during these months. Where are you from?" Siddharth asked, keeping his reading tablet down on the table.

"My name is Phil. I am originally from Missouri, USA. I am working as a language trainer at a Tibetan school in Mcleodganj. What about you?"

"My name is Siddharth. I work as a language instructor at a community school in Shimla. I see we work in similar profiles," Siddharth acknowledged warmly.

"What languages do you teach?"

"Hindi and English. I have been working for the last eight years. I am originally from Punjab."

"Hindi, you said? I have been working on my Hindi for quite some time now. My maid is teaching me Devanagari script. I learn the alphabet with her daughter. It is funny—we both started learning at the same time, but now she is ahead!" he remarked wittily, with a broad smile.

"I can understand. It takes time, especially when it is not your native language," Siddharth replied.

"I am still struggling with the *maatras*!" Phil exclaimed, making a sore face.

"You will get there. Don't worry," Siddharth reassured smilingly.

"I am going to order a cup of warm cocoa. Do you need anything?" Phil asked.

"No, please, go ahead," Siddharth replied. He picked up his tablet and resumed reading.

The café had cozy interiors. Most patrons sat hunched over the tables. They were either reading or indulging in low-pitched conversations. A strong undertow flowed in the river outside the place. It tenaciously swept past the boulder size rocks and made a resonant splashing noise.

"What are you reading?" Phil asked curiously.

"My article got published yesterday. I was reading the comments. You see, it has been ages since I got published. I am eager to know whether I am still any good, or not."

"That is so cool, man! What is it about?"

"The search for individual identity and understanding human relationships—through reading and viewing artistic representations, mainly."

"That is deep. You seem quite conversant with the topic. It is a little erudite for me—so it sounds. Do you mind if I take a look at it?" Phil asked.

"Sure," Siddharth replied, handing over the tablet to Phil.

"Saaransh—what is that? I am hearing the word for the first time."

"Summary," Siddharth replied tersely.

"Summary?" Phil asked, confused.

"It is a Hindi word. I have used it as a proper noun here. The meaning translates into 'summary'. There is no better word that encapsulates the essence of what I have written."

"Summary—as in conclusion—of your search—journey, I meant. Right?" he asked doubtfully.

"Quite right," Siddharth nodded.

"Have you found it? The conclusion—your journey's end?"

"I am still looking for him," Siddharth replied ponderously.

"Him? Is your conclusion a person?" Phil was confounded.

"I am sorry—I meant *it*. I get carried away at times," Siddharth replied evasively. Phil was still unconvinced. An awkward silence ensued between the two of them.

"Have you ever thought of writing a book?" Phil asked.

"Everyday. I am struggling to finish a manuscript that I had abandoned writing a long time ago. I just cannot bring myself to finishing it," Siddharth sighed.

"Maybe your inspiration hasn't come yet. You should keep writing. This stuff reads extremely good," Phil said, scrolling down the article.

"Enough about me. What made you travel all the way from Missouri to here?" Siddharth asked, quickly changing the topic.

"Love," he replied softly, in a steely voice. His manner laid bare the firmness beneath his gestures.

"Love?" Siddharth asked.

"My girlfriend, Martha, and I are planning to get married next year. I am Jewish, and her family are hardline Catholics. She hasn't told them about me yet. They would never approve of the match. We plan to elope as soon as I have enough money for the ring," he replied.

"The ring?"

"The wedding ring. I promised Martha I would get her the best wedding ring, ever. We both are saving for it. She tells me she will be fine with anything I get her. She has been begging me to come back," Phil replied.

"Consider me an amateur in matters of the heart," Siddharth began cautiously, "but don't you think that a ring is immaterial—as long as you have each other?" he asked.

"Nothing comes free in this world. I told Martha the same. If you love someone, you have to suffer to make it come real. I am willing to walk every last mile on the planet to prove that my love is stronger than I am," Phil replied resolutely.

Siddharth was gripped with a familiar longing. He looked around and saw that many people had already left.

"You look bothered. Is everything alright?" Phil asked, seeing Siddharth shift uncomfortably in his chair.

"Me? No, I am fine. I—how old are you?" Siddharth asked abruptly.

"I will complete twenty-two this year."

"You remind me a great deal of someone I once knew when I was of the same age," Siddharth said. A faint smile crossed his face.

"You? Oh, wait. How could I have missed this earlier? That is a beautiful ring! I didn't know you were married!" Phil exclaimed in joy, seeing the shiny silver ring on Siddharth's finger.

"Separated. We have been living apart for the last ten years," Siddharth replied mildly. A disquieting hush fell over them.

"I am sorry," Phil said.

"No, there is no need for you to feel sorry. I don't have any dearth of love in my life. My students love me. I am very attached to my parents. And I still love my partner— even though we haven't spoken in years," Siddharth replied.

Phil gazed at him in wonder. They sat silently for some time. Phil called the waiter and asked for the cheque.

"I need to go now. My guesthouse is ready. I am staying at Tiger Eye Resort—it is right at the end of this street, near the Manu temple. I am leaving tomorrow evening at six," Phil said, fastening his backpack on his shoulders.

"It was great meeting you, Phil. I wish you all the best with whatever you plan to achieve in life," Siddharth expressed warmly, shaking hands with him.

"All the very best with your manuscript, man. I hope you find the inspiration to carry it forward." Phil departed with a smile.

* * *

"Mariam, I would like to check out tomorrow night at eight. I have a bus to catch at eleven. I will settle your account in the morning. I hope it doesn't rain tomorrow," Siddharth sighed, taking his room key from the desk at the reception.

"I will do that right away. How was your day, professor?" Mariam asked politely, scribbling a reminder in her register.

"It was fine, Mariam. Thanks for asking. I met an interesting young traveller today. He was from Missouri, USA. I finally have a good story to tell back in the village," Siddharth replied with a kind smile.

He was about to leave when he saw a half-knit green woolen garment in Mariam's seat at the reception. "That's a beautiful pattern, Mariam. For whom are you making this?" Siddharth asked, pausing his steps. The garment looked bright and elaborately detailed.

"My grandson," she replied, beamingly.

"My daughter and he are coming here next month. They live in Canada. I had been begging to get this wool from the market. They sell it very expensive here. I asked my cousin to get it from Kashmir. It feels nice and different," she replied, gently rubbing the wool between her fingers. "They call it cashmere."

"It looks nice and warm—just how you intend it to be. I am sure he will love it. You are lucky to have your kids visit you every year, Mariam. It is good to have a family," Siddharth said.

He stepped inside his room with heavy steps. He kept the keys on the table and slumped into a chair. His exhaustion from last night hadn't yet completely worn off. The night was approaching near. The last rays of sun squinted through the narrow blinds into the room.

He looked at his ring with wistful eyes. It had faithfully remained on his finger for all these years. He embraced it in love and remembrance. He got up with a sigh and gently opened the briefcase that lay on the table. Inside, he found his letters and the pages of manuscript bundled in a neat pile. The typewriter ink had etched itself comfortably on the paper. He picked up the first letter and began reading it—slowly and warmly.

Dearest,

Sensation is violence. Since the moment I first met you, I have been profoundly unsettled.

It is true that the canvas of History is mottled with thick, wet, repugnant stains of crimson. The porosity of canvas, much like human consciousness, allows the seething hatred and ensuing bloodshed to seep in much deeper than what appears on the surface. But there is no record of the violence cast by sensations that prey upon the human heart. No amount of recorded suffering will ever be a veritable source to lay bare the gripping sensation, the overreaching desire to hug and embrace, to melt and coalesce—the narcissism of creationists and destructionists alike—which plagues two people who are unexpectedly jolted into an amorous union.

Romantic love is a consuming force. When a man exits his spiritual and physical precincts to find solace into those of the other, his flight, which begins by lustful embraces—soaked in promises of everlasting fidelity—and consummates into the warm physical interiors, he finds the act liberating, the hollowness of the interiors re-assuring; because his weary spirit finds a cherished abode—the body of the lover. But when the lovers realize the physical limits of their outreach, they are not only bewildered but also frightened, and ultimately turn destructive. For love, with its ever-widening appetite to enter and conquer, is a parasite that gnaws at and feeds off of the growing restlessness of the lovers' spirits to ascend and transcend the physical and spiritual boundaries.

During my evening walks, there are days, especially during the rainy season, when I come across an amusing spectacle and find myself wrestling with my ineptitude to describe it in words. In the open ground, adjacent to the park where I take walks, the grocers from all over the city erect colorful tarpaulins on rusty metal poles, to sell their produce to the local people. In the aftermath of a rainy day, one can catch a whiff of the freshly washed vegetables and grow befuddled imagining all the brilliant hues of green, red, purple, and yellow, packed under the vast expanse of tarpaulins glowing amber in the light of small neon bulbs hanging by naked twisted wires. To a bemused spectator observing the sight in the puddles formed by rainwater, the entire spectacle would seem like brushstrokes of raging colors blending into each other against the muddy patch engulfing them. The sensation would rob him of his intellect. The poverty of language would astound him; the self-doubt would give way to countless sufferings, tender at first and oppressive in the next.

Until I lay my head onto your chest and looked into your twinkling eyes, I had always turned my gaze away from the aforementioned spectacle, for its overpowering beauty terrified me of my own ignorance. Your eyes have taught me a different language. Today, when I see the spectacle and feel my anxieties rushing to the gut, I borrow your gaze and feel myself slipping into an enchanting reverie, where everything makes perfect sense: romance may not be a cure for human limitation, but it is a panacea for the uncultured, the perpetual sufferers, and the hopeless wanderers.

Always,
Me

1

The Arrival

Music Diary (Hindustani Music - Note #7):
Type: Thumri
Date: 21 January 2003

'Thumri', a compositional variant of the Hindustani classical music, is characterized—just like any other composition in the Hindustani music—by a long 'alaap' (a rhythmically free improvisation on the rules of the raaga to lend it life and flesh out its characteristics); closely followed by a long slow-tempo vocal or instrumental improvisation; and set in pace by 'bandish' (a fixed composition set in the raaga), performed by sarangi and/or harmonium, tanpura, and tabla. Believed to be first patronized in the 'durbar' (court) of Nawab Wajid Ali Shah, around 18th Century A.D., 'thumri' was commonly performed by courtesans.

Generally referred to as "the lyric of Indian Classical Music", the style is deeply romantic, with erotic overtones, typically lamenting a lover's separation from his/her beloved, and eagerly waiting for their physical as well as spiritual union.

Saaransh put his pen down and read the last sentence again. It seemed strange that even after conjuring the right emotions to write about music as romantic as Thumri, the sentence left him cold and unimpressed.

He checked his cellphone. It was half past nine at night. He had a date in fifteen minutes. He quickly changed his pants; tucked in his shirt; rinsed his mouth, and neatly combed his hair. He then stood in front of the mirror gazing at his jawline. He gave a quick nod and hurriedly left the room.

"Mom, I will be out for an hour," he signaled while rushing out from the front door.

"Where are you going at this hour of the night?" his mother came marching behind him. She looked annoyed and suspicious.

"I am heading over to Maanika's place. She and her sister want me to help them decide the menu for tomorrow's dinner. Remember I told you about the big party they are hosting tomorrow night?" he said, keeping a straight face while fidgeting with his car keys. She knows I'm lying, he thought fearfully.

"Okay. Don't be late. I am not sleeping until you come back," she replied sternly, realizing she couldn't argue anymore standing barefoot in the biting cold.

"Cool." He rolled up the car windows; switched on the convector; and turned the key into the ignition. Before he could start, he heard a faint buzz on his phone.

"Hey, I was hoping if you could park your car in the market area, then maybe we could both go somewhere in my car. The thing is, I haven't decided on the place yet, and thought we could work something out, together"—the text read. That's odd, he thought. "Okay. I will be there in five minutes. See you"—he replied.

Why is he taking so long? He checked his watch. It was ten minutes to ten. There were no parked vehicles around.

He dropped another text asking how much longer it would take. "Almost there"—he replied.

In the meantime, his thoughts strayed towards what he was working on earlier. Why is only unfulfilled love romantic? One would find scores of songs and other artistic works dwelling over the sufferings of the heart—the pain of separation, the eagerly wait for the amorous union. What happens when the lover finally arrives?

A wide beam of light, from directly across the road, disrupted his train of thought, blinding him momentarily. He stepped down from the car and peered through the dense fog. It must be him, he thought. He locked his car and started walking towards the beam. Upon reaching, he nervously opened the car door, quickly slid inside, and made himself comfortable in the front seat.

"Damn! It's cold. So, where are we going?" he asked, blowing heat into his cupped hands.

"Hi, let's start with the names, first," the person answered. Saaransh was stunned for a moment. He hadn't looked at the person until then. The voice had a pleasant ring to it—unlike of most people he met online. He turned his head to the right and gazed in astonishment. It was the most awkwardly built yet attractive face he had ever seen—bright and craggy, with a full smile stretching to the ears. There were puffy mounds, like cushions, below the eyes that twinkled when he spoke.

"Hi," Saaransh replied coyly. He immediately looked away. He wondered why he hadn't asked him for his picture before.

"Hi, my name is Akshay," Akshay replied, flashing his wide smile. Saaransh threw a quick, nervous glance at him. He noticed that the person had a cleft chain and tiny ears supported by a partially balding head. He strangely appeared both a little too old and young to be in his late twenties.

"Just take a left from here and then a right. I don't think you've ever been here before. It can be confusing at first, but it's terribly simple once you know the main checkpoints. I have a terrible sense of direction. I still use a map to find my way around in this city. Just imagine! Chandigarh is supposed to be among the most well-planned and carefully structured cities of the world. It's crazy, I know. Anyway, what's your name?" Saaransh went on unceasingly, trying his best to hide his nervousness.

"I already told you my name. My name is Akshay. I know my way around here. This city is my home. I was born and raised here," Akshay replied, confused.

"Oh, yeah. I'm sorry. I should have asked you first. My name is Saaransh," Saaransh replied sheepishly.

"So, what do you do, Saaransh? Your profile didn't mention any job roles. Are you still studying?" Akshay asked, quickly changing the subject.

"Well, I am going through a major career shift in my life right now. I recently managed to earn my Master's degree in Actuarial Sciences—finally! Early on in my course, I learnt I had no vocation for it. I am currently working as a journalist at The Indian Express. I had been interning with them during my college days. They were kind enough to give me a job," Saaransh replied.

"How old are you?" Akshay asked.

"I will be turning twenty-three this year."

"That's great! That must be too much effort, though. Not bad at all! Well, I am a software engineer. I am currently working as Senior Executive at Infosys, in Chandigarh. I must say I'm super impressed by your profile!" Akshay said, grinning cheerfully.

"Thank you. Yours is not any less impressive, either," Saaransh reciprocated the appreciation, wondering where the conversation was headed.

"You look different from the picture you sent me. I mean—don't get me wrong—you look much better—neat, maybe?" Akshay said, turning his eyes towards Saaransh, hoping to elicit an encouraging response.

"Thanks. You look great! I always had a thing for guys with grey hair—well, a few streaks of grey in the beard or on head, if not full grey," Saaransh replied cheerfully. I hope he doesn't think I am cheekily calling him old and shabby, he thought, biting his lower lip.

Akshay let out a chuckle. "I have never been described that way before. Thank you," he replied in good humor.
Akshay stretched his hand to eject the disc from the music player. Saaransh nervously pulled in his right knee closer, avoiding the intimate brush.

"So, what music do you like listening to?" Akshay asked.

"I am doing research work on Hindustani Classical music these days. The music has started to grow on me," Saaransh replied.

"My God! I have no such rarefied tastes in music. And I have no stock of it—or anything even remotely similar—on my phone! I hope you don't mind listening to Whitney Houston?" he asked, half-expectantly, in a worrying tone.

Saaransh was curiously taken aback by the over-reaction. "I am absolutely fine with it! I only said that because you asked. I am cool with whatever music you want to play. Whitney is my favorite, too," he said.

"Phew!" Akshay sighed. He pushed his chest back in a little and gave a sidelong, self-reassuring smile.

"Are you seeing anyone?" Saaransh asked. The question took him by surprise. He had no idea from where it had sprung up and how he made himself say that. It burst out of him, like some implacable urge that couldn't be tamed for long.

Akshay took a moment to answer. He pondered over it for a few seconds and then said, "That depends." Neither knew what that meant.

"Depends on...?" Saaransh asked. There was a brief pause.

"I am not sure...I have never been in love with anyone before...I don't think I can. My friends, who have been in love, tell me how beautiful it is. I can only be with someone if he gives me the assurance that he would be with me forever. It's forever, or simply not. I am not frivolous. I take matters of the heart seriously."

Saaransh was enamored. Akshay's response sounded like a solemn plea desperately clinging to the fantasy of love. It was tempered by childlike innocence and hardened by mature will. He appeared guarded and sounded endearingly contradictory.

"I want to see you again," Saaransh said, in a bemused tone, looking at him.

"Why?" Akshay asked.

"I don't know," Saaransh replied, unable to take his eyes off him.

"You don't know?"

"I don't know..."

Something stirred in the air. A balance was disturbed. Akshay swerved his car around the corner and took a U-turn, driving his way back.

"Are you alright? What happened? Are we going back?" Saaransh asked alarmingly, jolted from the impact.

"But what if you're hurt?" Akshay asked, with a startling urgency in his voice.

"Hurt by what?" Saaransh was perplexed.

"Heartbreak."

"I don't think I ever will be, as long as you are with me," Saaransh replied, letting his guard down at last. "What if you're hurt?" he asked, after a moment of reflection.

Akshay drove on silently with his eyes locked on the road ahead. "I think I will listen to a few of Whitney's songs, cry for a month, and then finally get over it," he replied with a crooked smile. His face was beginning to light up with a crackling radiance.

"Only a month? I am disappointed," Saaransh said teasingly.

Akshay grinned. They reached the spot where Saaransh had parked his car.

"Are we meeting again?" Saaransh asked.

"I don't know," Akshay sighed.

"You don't know?"

"I don't know..."

"I will be waiting. Bye."

Dearest,

His name was Jacky. Jacky, the evil dog, the wrongdoer and the monster, the re-telling of whose heinous deeds came to every parent's aid whenever his/her child ignored the deadline to reach back home before the nightfall.

I still remember the angry heat of bludgeoning June, hiding behind the stinky bushes overlooking Sarabjit uncle's house, to catch a glimpse of the mad, ailing dog. Dhruv, my cousin, who was two years younger than me but braver, always had a stone ready in hand if the beast decided to pounce on us. The rattle of chains signaled that the angry dog was coming to have his daytime fill from the wooden pail that his master would re-fill thrice a day. Uday, the panic-monger, the fat kid who wore big Bata shoes, would keep us all on our toes, in case the beast decided to show up earlier than its regular time. At last, the beast would come. A stench, which we later found out to be of dead animals, would issue from the surroundings, as if the odors waited long enough for their perpetrator to set them free.

The malignant beast that thronged our night-bound consciousness and inspired sheer terror even in sleep would come in tired spirits. The dull, large patch on his brown skin that separated itself from the rest of his body indicated the pace at which his skin was decaying, and decaying fast. Many people said that he had lived past his age and could die anytime. The rumors circulated for quite some time but none proved to be true as Jacky survived for more years than anyone claimed he would.

Compulsively, he would snap his angry jaws in a restless manner, as if he could always sense someone spying on him, and after staring fixedly at the bush for a few minutes, would turn away, drink his fill quietly and leave without a sound. None of us could ever reason why we went there every off and on or why the creature inspired such dread among us.

But as it is, one never realizes how closely one is attached to something until that something vanishes forever.

Then one day Jacky died. I distinctly remember sitting in the verandah with Dhruv, when we saw Sarabjit uncle lumbering through the sticky August monsoon with a loose leash rattling in dirt and gravel behind him. That was our first encounter with loss.

Something changed. My meals became shorter; I became more withdrawn; I started going to bed early, crying silently to sleep. And whenever grief became too great to bear, the stench, the same stench of rotten flesh would pervade my senses. Human beings are creatures of habit. The stench was my way of remembering Jacky. I didn't love him, but something about his decaying facade and hungry eyes reminded me of my own impermanence, of my own lust for survival. The stench became my stench. It is his odor that swims in my fluids. It is his grief that I cry for. It is his hunger that I lust after. There's a passage in me, a naked isolation, a maddening infinity that is beyond perception, beyond touch, beyond you and me.

Always,
Me

2

The Lives of Others

Saaransh sat silently at his desk with his feet upon the paperwork spilled across it. He was contemplating the events of last night. Would it be right to see him again? He thought. He had already told Akshay he would be joining him on the weekend. The meeting had changed something inside him. He was strangely unsettled. He rang up Maanika.

"Hey, still sleeping?" he asked.

"Saaransh, it's seven in the morning. What do you expect me to do? Do you ever sleep? This writing business is screwing with your head. Anyway, what happened?" she answered groggily.

"Whom am I supposed to call at this hour if not my best friend?"

"Saaransh, I am very sleepy. Will you please get to the point now? What happened?"

"Nothing. Well, actually, yes—but I am not sure how to put it," he replied.

"I am listening."

"I went out with someone last night. I told mom I was leaving for your place. I made up a story about you needing help with deciding tonight's menu for the party. Please handle her if she ever discusses this with you."

"What? Again? I am tired of being your scapegoat for everything! You called me up for this?"

"No—as I was saying, I went out with someone last night. Maanika, I have never been this affected by anyone before. I couldn't sleep a wink last night. He is the most charming person I've met so far!"

"Are you sure it's not another infatuation? I've seen you act like a maniac before. I don't want you to go there again. You're frightful when you do that!"

"Well, that was a long time ago. I suppose we all grow up somewhere, don't we? Besides, my sense of discrimination has tremendously improved! I know when it's infatuation and when it's—"

"It's what? Love?"

"Look, all I am saying is, I met this guy and I really like him. Our conversation was sparkling! Do you think I should go out with him on this weekend?"

"What's stopping you?"

"I am nervous. I am afraid of getting close...so close that I lose myself."

"You've only met him once. I would suggest you go out and get to know him a little more. First impressions can be false, too, right? One doesn't fall in love with someone that easily. And if it's meant to happen, there's no force on earth, which could stop it from happening."

"You think so?"

"Think what?"

"That if it's meant to happen, it will happen?"

"You will know! Now please, I need to catch some sleep before I start the day. I only have half an hour. Bye!" she hung up abruptly.

* * *

Later the same afternoon, he received a text from Akshay —"All set for Saturday?" A smile cracked across his face.

A second text appeared within seconds—"I will have two of my very close friends joining us. I hope you don't mind? You'll have a good time, I promise. They are nice people." Saaransh felt mildly betrayed.

"I'm not sure whether I would fit in. I'd love to, but I was hoping for something more intimate"—he replied.

"Ah, so well, in case that won't happen, we both can. The only issue is I already promised them. Sorry, it skipped out of my mind. I should have informed you earlier."

"I'll come along then. I trust you."

There was a pause. Saaransh wished he hadn't typed the last sentence. Did I just go overboard? He thought. His mind started filling up with frantic thoughts. Why is he taking so long to reply? He felt outraged.

"Why...?" Akshay replied.

"I don't know...you seem like a person I can trust. Well, what can I say? I like being reckless, I suppose. I only hope you don't spike my drink and throw me on the pavement. I am cool with the rest."

Akshay replied in a series of hysterical emoticons—"I love your sense of humor."

Saaransh giggled. "Anyway, where are we going?"

"To a gay party!"—Akshay replied.

"You're joking, right?"

"Why would I be?"

"I have never been to one! I don't think I am ready."

"Just put on your dancing shoes and hop along!"

"I am a little skeptical...I don't want to be among a hoard of drunken men thrashing on each other—reveling in the democracy of their bestial urges. It's a disturbing picture."

"Gotcha! I was just kidding! Besides, you have some terrible notions about that."

Saaransh was hugely relieved.

"You almost had me there! Anyway, where are we going then?"

"You'll be surprised how I never run out of these! We are going to the Vintage. I was hoping to just chat over a couple of drinks, have a good time, and call it a night."

"That seems perfect. Do you mind giving a little background of your friends? It would only help me bond better, I suppose."

"Okay, so, Deven and Yusuf have been dating each other for a while now. Deven, forty, is a physiotherapist by profession. Also, he is my best friend. Yusuf, thirty-two, is currently studying Psychology at Delhi University. He met Deven exactly a year ago, and the two of them have been going quite steady since then."

"They sound very interesting. I can't wait to see you guys. Will you be coming to pick me up?"

"Yeah, sure. I will call you before leaving. Be ready by six. It's a date."

"It's a date. See you very soon."

* * *

The evening sky appeared somber, with a dull milky hue slowly waning into the darkness that preludes night. A grey mist overhung the city. Dead leaves rustled past the agitated vehicles. There was a commotion in the streets. The blowing cold muffled the noises. Neons flickered. The evening gradually receded and nocturnal hours began to chime in.

"So, Akshay tells me you have a Master's degree in Actuarial Sciences," Yusuf said, looking in Akshay's direction, "and you work as a journalist at some newspaper company. Now that's something one doesn't get to hear often." His smile was infectious.

"Well, that's not very unusual. We have people working from all sorts of backgrounds. You see, I never possessed a knack for crunching numbers. I realized that early. I had previously interned at The Indian Express and those people were impressed with my work. Moreover, writing has always been my calling. I am in constant amazement of the art and the process," Saaransh replied coolly. Yusuf and Akshay nodded at each other in some shared understanding.

"Is this place usually this vacant?" Saaransh asked, turning his head around. It was an awfully quiet and scantly populated pub.

"Well, not many people know about it yet. It has just opened. They serve different variety of beer. Do you want to try?" Akshay asked.

"No, I don't drink beer. I hate the smell," Saaransh replied.

"Oh, I didn't know that. I can get you something else if you like? I ordered wheat beer for all of us while you were in the loo," Akshay replied.

"No, I am fine with gin and pineapple juice. I can't handle alcohol," Saaransh said smilingly. There was a nervous exchange between the two of them. They felt they were being observed. Both took great care in avoiding any physical brush. Every time Saaransh caught Akshay stealing a glance at him, Akshay looked away embarrassingly, joining in the conversation with more vigor than before.

"Perhaps you two would like to be left alone for some time. Deven and I are sorry for ruining your date," Yusuf said teasingly.

"No—" Saaransh and Akshay both protested at the same time. They looked at each other, flushed with embarrassment. The distance between the two was fraught with tense energy and awkward silence, resisting the invisible pull of unabashed intimacy.

"There you are," Yusuf grinned. "Deven, honey, why don't you say something? Shall we leave the two love birds alone?" Yusuf said, nuzzling Deven's resting head against his shoulder with his cheek. Deven had been quiet the whole evening. He appeared brooding, with his gaze intent on Saaransh. All through the evening, he had barely left hold of Yusuf's hand. The two seemed inseparable. Saaransh thought perhaps his presence was undesired and irked Deven.

"No, it's completely fine. I am really liking everyone's company," Saaransh reassured smilingly, brushing away awkwardness.

"If you say so," Yusuf said, tilting his head in amusement.

"Look, the drinks are here," Akshay said, pointing in the direction of the waiter. Everyone was distracted.

"You two really complement each other," Saaransh said, addressing Deven and Yusuf.

The compliment seemed to be working with Deven. A smile appeared at the corner of his lips. He moved his hand up against Yusuf's thigh and leaned in his face a little closer to his chest. Saaransh was relieved that Deven was finally warming up to him.

"Deven had almost given up hope that he would find anyone. But nothing could be better timed and opportune than our first meeting. We met online—just like you two did. I was struggling with a failed relationship and a job in advertising that sucked the life out of me. Deven had recently become a Buddhist, renouncing all material desires. He wasn't even looking for a date. We were chatting casually when we decided to meet, and boom! It happened. Just like that," Yusuf went on excitedly, with bursts of animation.

Saaransh and Akshay could feel the distance between them shrinking.

"How does it work, then? I mean, do you guys ever argue or fight?" Saaransh inquired patiently.

"You see—"

"Anything that is romantic is turbulent," Deven replied calmly, cutting Yusuf before he could even begin. Deven seemed unperturbed, with his head comfortably leaned against Yusuf's chest. The utterance had a resounding effect. His voice, despite its softness, carried a ringing authority that annihilated all doubt. They both embraced each other reassuringly. Their lives seemed suspended yet moving in a singular frame where every shared silence and touch quelled the storm in their hearts.

"Why don't we head over to my place after the drinks?" Yusuf asked.

"I am not sure...I have to reach home early," Saaransh demurred.

"Come. For me," Akshay said, looking at him directly in the eyes.

"Alright," Saaransh replied, captivated by his firmness.

* * *

"So, how was it?" Maanika asked teasingly, in mock amusement.

"You will have to patiently hear me out," Saaransh replied.

"I am always patient with you."

"I am not sure what to make of it. We were at his friend's place. The music was on. We were dancing together and embracing each other. And we shared a kiss. It was magical.

I have kissed a lot of people by now, but this was different. The moment my lips touched his, I could feel every nerve in my body relaxing. It wasn't wild or passionate—just sensual."

"That was quick, don't you think?"

"It wasn't a proper kiss. We withdrew from it, reluctantly. His friends started sniggering, you see."

"That must have been awkward."

"Not really. We were strangely aloof. I rested my head on his lap and he played with my hair for a little while. I just didn't want to leave, but then—"

He was cut short by a vibrating noise on his phone. It was a text from Akshay.

"Listen, I need to hang up now. I promise I will get back to you soon."

"Fine. Please do. I need to hear this." They both hung up.

"Am I just a passing phase for you?"—The text read. Saaransh didn't know how to respond. The question seemed abrupt, yet it had an urgency to it.

"You could be. I don't think so, to be honest. That's a hard question to answer. I have never felt, like I did today, ever in my life before. I think I could get used to you"—he replied optimistically.

"I like open ended answers. Somehow, it's not comfortable in our scenario, if you know what I mean."

Saaransh didn't know what Akshay meant. He didn't care about it, either. Suddenly, his insides began to churn. The air became densely suffocating. He wanted to scream in agony.

"I don't know what to say. It's all right, I guess. I can live with it."

"I'm sure you can."

Dearest,

My eyes hadn't seen a more vivid green like that of her nightgown; my nose hadn't yet smelled how unpleasant morning breath felt; my tongue hadn't tasted the salt of the night; my ears hadn't heard such indecipherable noise, and my skin hadn't felt the warmth of a nighttime hug. I was born in a taintless reel of life that acquired color and momentum from that single incident.

"*I've had enough. What sin did I commit in past life to deserve such a fate!*" *she sobbed.*

"*You think your life is hell? You have made things worse for everyone! Look at yourself!*" *the man retorted angrily.*

"*You should be thankful to me. If it hadn't been for my father, we would still be living without a roof over our heads! You ungrateful wretch!*"

"*Go! Take away everything. Don't believe even for an instant that we're all living on your charity.*"

"*I can go anytime I want. This is my house! You have no right to tell me when I should leave. I would have left years ago! But no, I still had hope! Hope that things would get better!*"

"*You think you're the only one who is suffering? I have been bearing your madness forever now! You can go and dig up space anywhere you like.*"

The argument seemed to be moving in a circle. It was exhausting to watch them accuse each other of similar things. My grandmother's anger knew no bounds; but she relaxed afterwards, slowly moving on to do household chores. My grandfather—the tall, strangely composed man—seemed mildly at ease after spitting fire for nearly half an hour. And thus, they resumed with their morning duties. It was a curious sight.

She kissed me on the cheek and asked for how long I had been awake. She then warmed some milk and poured it into a bleak, discolored mug. It tasted like sweat and sugar. And her gold bangles made a clinking noise whenever they touched the mug. It was the first that I tasted of her: resentment, like powdered chocolate swirling over the white mass of her buried desperation; and love, like sugar dissolving fast into the soluble liquid.

She talked of distant lands where the moon shone bright and nocturnal sounds filled the silent hours of the night; where the damp earth delighted in receiving the spaces between toes and the gentle breeze lovingly stroked the naked skin—her birthplace, she said. She pined after a lost lover. The only time she loved, she claimed and sighed despondently.

Music sustained her. It added color and taste to her life. For a brief moment, she would forget the touch of loose cloth flitting over her unyielding breasts. She crooned the melodies of love, lust, despair, promises of marital bliss, and pain of separation. It lent her an air of defiance—an otherworldly charm that unmoored her from the banal life that she was forced to lead.

I stood there watching when disease devoured her and the hour of death loomed near. Her mouth lay agape, foaming with streams of blood and tissue. Her body convulsed with every breath she labored to muster. Her eyes conveyed horror and desperation. The moist impression of her kiss on my cheek hadn't faded through the years. I gently rubbed her cheek and planted a kiss on her forehead. She passed away in the wee hours of the night.

Knowing love had made her life an aberration. She struggled and wept alone. The loneliness accompanied her till death. She once told me that there are no lives lost in love, but only martyred. The only sore losers are the ones who die without tasting their lovers' lips.

Always,
Me

3

The Kiss

"What does love mean to you?" the person asked.

It had been twelve days since the night he went out with Akshay—twelve inconsolable days. He sat at the coffee table with his arms folded across his chest. He appeared impassive and withdrawn. The person sitting opposite him was growing increasingly uneasy.

"Hey listen, I have to ask you this: Am I bothering you?" He arched his eyebrows, throwing a quizzical look.

"You—what?" Saaransh was distracted. His attention had been waning.

"Am I bothering you? I am not an expert at reading facial expressions, but you seem displeased and lost—I don't know where!"

"No...I am sorry. I had a tiring day at work. I am a little distracted at the moment. So, you were asking me something?" Saaransh replied, folding his hands and resting his arms on the table.

"Only if you say so," the person replied doubtfully. "I was asking what love means to you."

Saaransh cringed. He wondered how and when the conversation had reached the subject.

"I am a fatalist in love," he replied. "And a defeatist," he added after a pause.

"You don't believe in it then?"

"Believe in what?"
"The fantasy!" The person exclaimed in disbelief.
Saaransh shrugged his shoulders.
"Well, would you like to order anything else?" the person asked. He sounded disappointed.
"I think I am going to call it a night."

* * *

Saaransh exited the café, wrapping layers of woolen around his neck. He checked his cellphone. There were two missed calls from work and one from home. He slid it back inside and started walking towards the parking basement.

His gaze followed every couple that was walking hand in hand. He anxiously kept scanning every passerby for Akshay. He walked with quick steps, fighting the wringing sadness that was rising within him. He was haunted by a terrible loneliness. Darkness swept across his eyes. He felt as if he were walking into a narrowing abyss. The voices around him suddenly drowned in a deafening silence.

The basement was lit with halogens. The walls appeared charred and flaking in uneven patches. He found his car parked in a deserted corner. It was late. He could hear the sound of his footsteps reverberating through the corridor. There were very few cars around. He cut another call from home.

"Who were you with?" He heard an inebriated voice call out at him from behind. The voice sounded strangely familiar.

He turned around and saw Akshay slouched against a wall. He looked fatigued and untidy. He had an unsettling look on his face.

Saaransh was unable to respond. At first, he felt a relaxing sensation spread through his chest, soon replaced by hot flashing anger.

"Are you stalking me?"

"Answer me first!"

"You have no right to demand anything from me! How did you even get in here like this? What's wrong with you?" Saaransh retorted, pointing at Akshay's disheveled appearance.

"Who was that? Your new boyfriend?"

Saaransh shook his head in disbelief. He clapped his hands in the air and took a step back.

"You amaze me! It was you who backed out. You didn't want this! And now you come stalking all the way like a vengeful lover! Just go away. I don't want to see you again!" He bellowed.

Akshay simmered down. His face was contorted with remorse and guilt. He lowered his eyes apologetically. Saaransh turned his back on him spitefully and started walking towards his car with resolute steps.

"Saaransh, I am sorry. I got scared. I thought...I thought you were too good for me. Everything was happening so fast and I had never felt like that before. Please give me one more chance...I promise I will make it right this time."

Saaransh paused his steps and turned around.

"This is the second time I am faced with a situation like this. The first time it happened, I tried to console myself thinking it's part of life and my life had just begun. To be steadily optimistic by thinking I would find love someday seems more and more difficult with each passing day. This is what you meant the first time I talked about the world chopping my idealism. You said my ideals would remain the same, but the test will get difficult with each stage. I guess it has already begun. So, yeah, why am I hurt then? I shouldn't be, right? I should have seen this coming," Saaransh answered in a restrained voice. His manner was mild and incisive. His eyes were clouded with tears.

"Hey, are you crying?" Akshay asked worryingly, taking a step towards Saaransh.

"Just go away! Please...I am not so strong!" Saaransh burst into tears. His whole body convulsed with violent emotion. He banged his fists on the car and slumped down beside the door. His muffled sobs turned into wails of anguish.

Akshay knelt down beside him with a quick, impulsive movement. He held him by the shoulders and gently raised him up. Saaransh tugged at Akshay's shirt. He then looked at him questioningly and pushed him away.

"I can deal with being lonely, but I dread being abandoned," Saaransh said, composing himself. He had a determined look on his face. "Goodbye."

Saaransh was beginning to step inside his car when Akshay grabbed his hand and swerved him around. They both stared into each other's eyes. Their expressions read shock and burning desire. Akshay pulled Saaransh closer and pressed his mouth against his.

They locked in a passionate embrace. Saaransh grabbed Akshay by the collar and forced his tongue inside. Akshay pulled at Saaransh's waist, drawing his tongue deeper inside. They wrestled fiercely.

Saaransh could feel his lips turning sore and strength diminishing. He relaxed his hold on Akshay and gently cupped his hands around Akshay's face. Akshay slowed down. He could feel familiar warmth rising inside him. He put his arms around Saaransh's waist and kissed him slowly, tenderly nibbling at his lower lip.

Time stood still. Saaransh could hear the breeze whistling past his ears. Suddenly their situation dawned on him. He withdrew immediately.

"Akshay, people might be watching," he expressed in a concerned voice.

"Let them," Akshay replied. He was unrelenting. He pulled him close again, unwilling to let go.

"No, wait!" Saaransh gently pushed him back.

"You know, the first time I saw you, I knew I couldn't do without you. You scared me. I wouldn't have dared asked you out. And I couldn't be more grateful that you did," Akshay said, taking Saaransh's hand in his hand and gently kissing it.

"Where are we going with this?" Saaransh asked.

Akshay looked at him, smiling dimly. He caressed his cheek and with twinkling eyes, replied, "To the stars."

Dearest,

Perhaps it is true that even today all possible feelings do not yet exist. They lie on some outward surface, beyond time and space, waiting to be kindled. And every time when love shines in the world, a new feeling is born.

There was once a lady called Ami Azan, who suffered from night terrors and episodes of mania. Her shrill cries ran through the neighborhood. She was an impious lady. She had committed a terrible sin, they said. May Allah have mercy on her soul! No one had seen her for years. She lived alone with her mother in disgrace.

Once Ami Azan noticed a shaft of light breaking through a thin crevice of the unhinged door. She clutched at her breasts. She heard the distant noise and chatter of children running and playing in wild excitement. The sound filled her with ecstasy. It soon started pelting at her mercilessly. She shrank back in horror.

All her life she had bemoaned the dearth of music. She remembered a time in her early adulthood when her proximity to young nascent bodies enraptured her greatly. Their sweet albeit discordant sounds aligned with her entrails. She remained hidden behind their duality. Their music echoed in her ripe bosom.

"I am worried for you, dear," her mother said. "You must go out. The world is not unforgiving. You have suffered enough."

She stared fixedly at the shaft of light. It advanced towards her softly. She crawled back. Her eyes conveyed sorrow and emptiness.

"You must pray with me. Allah has forgiven you."

Then one day Ami Azan stepped out at dawn. She heard a mystifying aural symphony in the air. She took out her prayer mat and started walking barefoot towards the masjid. Her hair streamed behind her as she walked leaning on a jagged wooden stick. The pewter sky smiled at her. The sound of Imam offering prayers beckoned to her. Naive birds awakened by the first light of dawn flapped their silver wings furiously. She spread her mat on the pristine floor, wrapped the hijab around her head, and with hands joined in worship started murmuring fervent prayers to Allah. Her fears metamorphosed into tears of gratitude. She held her breasts in delight. She looked at the sky and blinked with wonder. A new feeling was thus born in the history of time.

Perhaps love is some master musician. It orchestrates life forces to surrender and conjoin. It annihilates distinction.

The indistinct chords promise the fine-tune of harmony, of melody, of strings, flutes, clarinets, and voices working in perfect order; while the distinct chords, forever straining under love's adept fingers, revolt against the oppressive order; their harsh, inconsonant sounds in the milieu of musical grandiosity, struggle to remain stiff and alone, but alas, they must give away, love argues; thus love beats one more time, and the chords, both distinct and indistinct, sounding the beat of pleasure and pain, reach a crescendo; love smiles, a new symphony is thus born.

Some sensations are yet to be discovered. Some symphonies lie hidden in the naked crevices of our bodies. Thus, we two distinct chords, forever bereft and dissonant, collide, struggle, kiss, tear, gnaw, and perspire, till we meld and resonate.

We beat on, in flesh and spirit.

Always,
Me

4

An Equal Music

"Mom, where is that Sahir Ludhianvi disc that I gifted you on your last birthday?" Saaransh called out to his mother. He was getting annoyed rummaging through the old music records. The dust was starting to bother him.

"Have you ever considered cleaning this mess?" he grumbled, trying to suppress a sneeze.

"Only if you could lend me some help. I can't do this all by myself! Why don't you clean it up right now?" His mother answered while coming out of the kitchen.

"Here, take this." She handed him a towel to dust off the shelves.

"Have you seen the disc? I have been looking for it since last night. I thought you were listening to it a few days ago."

"It must be in the drawer. Did you look in there? I always keep them back in their boxes."

"Which drawer?"

"The one you're leaning on."

Saaransh opened the drawer and found the disc box right on top. He was embarrassed.

"Since last night you said?" she taunted.

"Okay, fine! My sinuses were getting irritated by all the dust here!" He retorted in defense.

"Do you remember that song written by Sahir Ludhianvi, which grandma sang on her seventeeth birthday? It goes like—*Tujhe aur ki tamannah mujhe teri aarzoo hai,*" he intoned. "I can't recall the rest."

"Oh, yes—*Jise tu qubool kar le*—from Bimal Roy's *Devdas*. What a beautiful movie! Dilip Kumar moved audiences to tears in it! Such a brilliant performer! There has never been an equal," she sighed with nostalgia.

"Yeah. I remember you telling me about it when we went for Bhansali's *Devdas*. Lost in opulence—you bitterly remarked. I was taken in by the spectacle, though. The performances were great, too. I wonder why you would say that," Saaransh replied, taking out a thin booklet from the disc box. He flipped through the pages and found the lyrics to the song that he was looking for.

"That's because you haven't seen Bimal Roy's version yet," she sneered with condescension. "Anyway, why are you asking about the song?"

"Well, Akshay and I are going to a musical soirée tonight, and I was hoping to prepare something just in case I am called on to sing. You know how Maanika keeps poking fun at my singing! She will make sure everyone knows about it!" Saaransh replied.

"Why don't you pick something simpler? Besides, I don't think the song would fit the ambience. It's a little gloomy...and very old," she replied, skeptical.

"Well, I don't intend to sing it, actually. You remember the paper I was writing on Hindustani Classical music? I have decided to take a short break and work on English translations. I have fond memories of grandma singing that song—since it was her last birthday then. I thought it would be nice to begin from there."

"You've been keeping up with that? I thought you had stopped translating long ago."

"I want to pick it up again. I am getting nowhere on my paper. I need to take some time off and get some inspiration, mom."

"Fine." She relented nonchalantly, arranging the disc boxes.

"This is a particularly tricky translation," he said, reading from the booklet. "Help me here, my memory is a little rusty. So, the lovelorn courtesan implores her beloved weary patron by singing—*Jise tu qubool kar le woh adaa kahaan se laaun—*, which translates as 'From where shall I summon the charm that you shall accept'. Sounds right, uh?" he asked doubtfully, looking up.

"Graciously accept," she remarked.

"Do you think I should go with the literal word by word translation? Or just translate the essence of the verse—like paraphrasing?" he asked.

"What have you been doing earlier?"

"Word by word, mostly. Those translations were simpler. This is a little tricky."

"Well, you can't compromise on the essence, though. Why don't you start penning it down? You have the right start, at least."

"Okay. Cool. I will be back. I am going to the park. Leave the top three shelves for me. I will clean them once I am done."

<u>Music Diary (Translation #103)</u>:
Song: Jise Tu Qubool Kar Le
Movie: Devdas (1955)
Music Director: Sachin Dev Burman
Lyricist: Sahir Ludhianvi
Translation Language: English

Jise tu qubool kar le
Woh adaa kahaan se laaun
Tere dil ko jo lubhaa le

Woh sadaa kahaan se laaun

(That what you shall graciously accept
From where shall I summon that charm
That what delights your heart
From where shall I summon that skill)

Main woh phool hoon ke jisko
Gayaa har koi masal ke
Meri umr beh gayi hai
Mere aansuon mein dhal ke

(I am that innocent blossom
That everyone has trampled upon
My life has been washed away
In the tears I have shed)

Jo bahaar ban ke barse
Woh ghataa kahaan se laaun
Tere dil ko jo lubhaa le
Woh sadaa kahaan se laaun

(That what showers like spring
From where shall I summon that dark cloud
That what delights your heart
From where shall I summon that skill)

Tujhe aur ki tamannah
Mujhe teri aarzoo hai
Tere dil mein gham he gham hai
Mere dil mein tu he tu hai

(You desire someone else
I yearn for you

Your heart is only full of sorrow
My heart is only full of you)

Jo dilon ko chain de
Woh dawaa kahaan se laaun
Tere dil ko jo lubhaa le
Woh sadaa kahaan se laaun

(That what relieves the despairing hearts
From where shall I summon that cure
That what delights your heart
From where shall I summon that skill)

Meri bebasi hai zaahir
Meri aah-e-be-asar se
Kabhi maut bhi jo maangi
Toh naa paayi uske dar se

(My helplessness is revealed
Through my empty sighs
Even when I have begged for death
I have not been granted from His doorstep)

Jo muraad le ke aaye
Woh dua kahaan se laaun
Tere dil ko jo lubhaa le
Woh sadaa kahaan se laaun

(That what fulfills my ardent wish
From where shall I summon that prayer
That what delights your heart
From where shall I summon that skill)

"Hi, honey. Getting ready for tonight?" Saaransh put the

pen down and answered his phone.

"Hey, can we meet right now?" Akshay asked.

"Why? Is everything alright?"

"Yeah, I just wanted to make you listen to something."

"Right now? Can't we do this later? You don't have to come all the way to see me for this. We are meeting tonight anyway."

"Just for fifteen minutes, please. I was driving by your sector. I don't think I would be comfortable sharing it with Maanika in the car."

"Uh—okay. I am sitting in the park right opposite my house. Be quick. I have promised mom that I would help her clean the music cupboard."

"I am right behind you."

Saaransh turned around and saw Akshay waving at him from inside his car. He hurriedly got up and ran towards it.

"What's the emergency?" he asked. He kept his diary in the empty space near the gearbox and locked the door.

"Ever heard of Nina Simone?" Akshay asked.

"No. Is she an actress?"

"I am amazed! You keep talking about music all the time and you don't know one of the leading Jazz vocalists and composers of all time!"

"Correction: I listen to only Indian music. I am quite ignorant about the rest. And since when did you start listening to Jazz?"

"I love Jazz! It's just we never got around to talking about it."

"What a terrible lover I am! I can't believe it's been four months and I had no clue about your favorite music genre. I had assumed you listened to more—pop?"

"There's plenty more you haven't seen—or tasted" He rolled his eyes mischievously, pointing to his jeans.

"You're sick! I am leaving."

"No! Wait. I was kidding, love!" Akshay pulled him back inside.

"Your five minutes are up. Hurry! Mom doesn't know I am with you."

"Okay, just close your eyes. I am playing something for you. I want you to listen to it with full attention."

Saaransh complied unwillingly.

"No cheating," Akshay admonished. "And feign interest for me, please."

Saaransh heard a soft, whisky-soaked voice streaming from the music player. He was disarmed. The voice was subdued, plaintive and yet achingly beautiful.

"Honey, this is won—"

"*Shhh*, listen," Akshay hushed him.

I love you, Porgy
Don't let him take me
Don't let him handle me
And drive me mad

"Nina's father tells a young Nina that someday they both will travel the world and see distant places. Nina will experience her share of joys and sorrows—like everyone else—and see that deep down we are all same," Akshay began.

Don't let him handle me
With his hot hands
If you can keep me
I want to stay here with you, forever
I've got my man

"Nina becomes a pianist and tours the whole world—like her father said. She searches for love in distant lands. Soon she becomes increasingly despondent and disillusioned, as wherever she went there was no Porgy—someone to love her. Then one day she goes to Africa and there she falls hopelessly in love with a crippled man, called Porgy."

Someday I know he's coming to call me
He's going to handle me and hold me
So, it's going to be like dying, Porgy
When he calls me
But when he comes I know I'll have to go

"Back in America, she shares an abusive relationship with a drug dealer who forces her to come back. Nina later regrets going back to America, leaving behind Porgy. She doesn't want to go, but instead wants to stay with him."

If you can keep me
I wanna stay with you, forever
I've got my man

"Nina always knew that her love was ephemeral. She knew that she would have to return and suffer the indignities that she had always endured—but her falling in love was inevitable. She pleads Porgy to keep her back with him and never let her go away."

Akshay took Saaransh's hand in his hand, and continued, "Now open your eyes, slowly."

Saaransh was spellbound. He looked at Akshay with searching eyes and began—"Akshay, I don't know what to say..."

"I just want you to remember that no matter where we are tomorrow, or who we are with, you and I shared this together—just you and me, alone. We made this journey which no else did." He kissed Saaransh on his forehead and with smiling eyes said, "I love you, Saaransh. I don't want to ever lose you. I don't know what my life would be without you."

Saaransh lovingly reciprocated him with a tight hug. "I have a feeling you are going to mess up my whole life," he said, slightly shaking his head.

"A little mess has never harmed anyone." Akshay stroked Saaransh's chin gently.

Saaransh smiled. "Now go before people see us like this. You are in a colony, remember?"

"You have a knack for killing the romance just when it begins," Akshay whined, taking his hands off of Saaransh.

Saaransh grinned. "Now go. Don't be late tonight. Maanika and I will be waiting." He left in haste, leaving his diary behind.

* * *

The air was soaked with cordial whisper and music. The entire lobby was suspended in a scarlet mist. There was an unmistakable drone that punctuated the muted ambience. Fairy lights shone dimly against minimalist wall patterns. Cocktail glasses clinked occasionally.

"Maanika, I don't think Akshay would like it here. I mean, he doesn't listen to Indian music. He wouldn't be able to appreciate much," Saaransh said.

The homegrown music audience sat around a makeshift raised platform. They exuded bonhomie and recited themes of the day. Poets and singers took turns at the karaoke. There was frequent clapping in a display of solidarity and genuine praise.

"You guys have been going out for a long time now. The least you could have done is made him listen to good Indian music," she remarked casually, adjusting her dupatta.

"I didn't even know he liked listening to Jazz, until this afternoon. We never broached the subject. Will you stop fidgeting with your dupatta?" Saaransh was getting annoyed.

"It's your fault! You told me the theme was ethnic. Look around you—there is no one else wearing a suit!" She retorted irritably.

"Ethnic doesn't only cover suits and saris, besides—wait, where is Akshay?" He realized Akshay had been gone for a long time. "He said he was going to the loo. It has been some time now. Do you think he left?" he asked worryingly.

"No, don't over-react. He must be around. Just go and check. I want to listen to the next performer. He has got such a charming voice!" She clapped her hands gleefully.

Saaransh went around looking for Akshay in the crowd, greeting every familiar face with a polite nod. He was getting weary of the niceties. At last, he found Akshay engrossed in conversation with a young scholarly looking gentleman dressed in white attire. Akshay talked with surprising ease, smiling occasionally. Saaransh was stung. He stood there noting his every gesture. Soon he walked away, mildly disgusted.

"Hey Maanika, have you seen Saaransh?" Akshay asked, excusing himself to the passersby as he jostled towards her.

"He had gone looking for you some thirty minutes ago," Maanika replied.

"I was talking to a guy about Saaransh's work. You know—the music diary he is maintaining. This gentleman seemed to know a great deal about Indian Classical music. I approached him casually. I picked up a few things about the subject while talking to him."

"Hasn't he taken some time off it recently?"

"Yeah, he told me about that. Listen, I will just go and see where he is. He is not even taking my calls."

Akshay found Saaransh at the cocktail lounge, leaned against the counter.

"Saaransh, where have you been? I was looking for you—is that alcohol? You know it doesn't agree with you, love," Akshay said politely, taking the wine glass off his hand.

"*Shhh, mujhe jaan naa kaho meri jaan,*" Saaransh hushed him in a drunken voice, rounding his lips with every syllable. "Don't call me your life, oh, my life." He leaned against Akshay, fondling his back with amorous strokes.

"You're not going home like this. I promised your mom I would take care of you. Come with me." Akshay held Saaransh firmly by the hand and dragged him out of the lobby. Stares followed, voices murmured.

"Sit here while I go back inside and get you something," he said, pointing to a couch.

Saaransh clutched at his hand and pulled him closer. "Why do you get so scared? Why do you act so perfect? We haven't even touched each other yet. Don't you want to know what's here?" Saaransh said, slowly unbuttoning his shirt. Akshay stopped him immediately.

"Saaransh, you're drunk. I am not doing this with you. Don't force me to—"

"Force you to what?" Saaransh replied haughtily, leaping from the couch in quick anger.

Akshay lost his nerve. He pushed him back violently. In one quick movement, he unbuttoned the top two buttons of his shirt, took off his shoes, and pounced on Saaransh. He held him down with brute strength.

Saaransh was knocked back into his senses. He was frightened to see Akshay behave like that.

"Akshay, what are you—"

"*Shhh, meri bebasi hai zaahir, meri aah-e-be-asar se,*"

Akshay mumbled, grazing his nose along Saaransh's neck. Saaransh could feel Akshay's hot breath on his skin.

"Wait, but how—have you been reading my diary?" He was confounded. He was surprised to hear Akshay recite the lyrics he had been working on in the afternoon.

Akshay laid silently with his lips pressed against Saaransh's neck. He relaxed his hold on him. Saaransh was flustered.

"I don't understand, honey. What's bothering you?" Saaransh asked, watching him get up and casually button his shirt.

"*Jo muraad le ke aaye, woh dua kahaan se laaun.* From where shall I summon the prayer that fulfills my ardent wish," Akshay intoned.

"I still do not—"

"When was the last time you told me you loved me? When did you ever say that?" His voice was tremulous. He looked at Saaransh with questioning eyes. Saaransh was hurt.

"Why do you want me to say it vocally? I say it all the time—in gestures, in things I do for you!" Saaransh defended himself.

"You know what, I give you all the assurances without your asking. It just seems...seems like...like you take me for granted. Maybe it would be nice to say once in a while that you care, that you love me."

Saaransh's eyes welled with tears. He couldn't defend himself against the accusation. He knew Akshay was hurt. Nothing else mattered to him.

"Now wait here while I get you something. Don't let anyone else come in," Akshay said in a controlled voice, restraining his anger and disappointment.

He was beginning to leave when Saaransh came running and hugged him from behind. He was disarmed. He felt his whole body melting in the tight embrace.

"I love you. I will say it a thousand times if I have to. I love you. I love you—my Porgy."

Dearest,

I write this letter to you in earnest. Hopelessness and frustration plague me. I plead your mercy. I seek your urgent help.

Metro-station. I hear the footfall of hundreds of passengers. A continuum of actively congregating genitals—both limp and firm—vigorously engaging in the commerce of everyday life. Sweat and sound.

They rejoice in the tight economy of space. Life has prepared them for it. Industrious hands. A man gropes me from behind. I am pushed against an iron pole. He says he means no harm. He regrets being held up here. We all do. I feel his tightness between my legs. He pleads me to touch it, once. Sure. I rub my hands against it. He says he likes it. His wife wouldn't do it for him. He says he is sorry. He begs me to put it in my mouth. I love you, he says. He pleads with despairing eyes. His chipped nails are dyed blue. He pulls my hair back and enters my throat.

I am sprawled on the greasy floor. The train rattles. People come and leave. I am jealous of my invader's strength. I clasp my hands behind his neck. He stokes me with all his might. Toothless grins follow. A woman gasps in horror. She reaches for her organ. She is dismayed at her own fragile mechanism. The man moans loudly. He is disgusted, he says. He is revolting.

A youth forces my face between his thighs. He is tired of submitting to older men. They all mistreat him. He is tired of playing to their fantasies. He asks me if I like it. I do. Naïve. Hasty. He loosens his grip. Hairs on his groin prick my tongue. An old man yawns. Flabby and flaccid. He has seen far too much to care. He gazes nonchalantly.

They say they want to enter me. I guard my flesh against their weapons. You have done it with them. Submit to us, they shout. They tie me on a leash and spit on my face. I revel in their abuse. There is very little to enter, they moan. Spit and semen surround me. The putrid stench mixes with my own odor.

Yet I am free, I argue. I am alive. The burden both shocks and amuses me. I impregnate the thin air with the saliva I blow. I let the warmth of urine spread across my inner thigh. I am in command of my body. I own the space. I own the vacuum. I am here, more than anywhere. The train stops.

I get down from the train. I walk bruised and ragged. A daft figure looks at me with manic eyes. He has borne the brunt of life. His life has been a curse. He flails on the shores of memory. He tries to scare me. I walk on, unaffected. Soon he retreats from his labor. He must let me go. Letting go comes to him easily. He has let go of many things. His memory fails him.

The streets are amassed with people of all hues and scents. I find their touch and smell revolting. I am oppressed by my free will. I am trapped in my body. I breathe in and out into myself. Children defecate in the open drains. They balance their bodies with precision. Their sordid mess drops into the rushing sewer. They smile at me. I smile back.

My desires revolt me. My flesh bears the scourge of a thousand natural shocks. Yet I persist. I perspire, unknowingly victim to my instincts.

Deliver me from my burden. Liberate me. Save me from the rotting stench that I am.

Always,
Me

5

Lust

Phagwara. Interior Punjab. Angry sunlight hammered against the car windows. Dark clouds of smoke billowed from soot-crusted industrial chimneys. The road was assailed by ruptured tar and smears of cow dung. Potholes sent the heads crashing against the roof.

"How much farther, dad?" Saaransh asked.

"I don't know. I am coming here after fifteen years," his father answered. "The place hasn't changed much," he said in a dejected tone.

Open sewers ran along the decrepit structures that bordered narrow roads. Traffic clogged the streets. Flies festered.

"You picked the money from the table, right?" His mother asked his father.

"I did. Remember, just an hour—no more, no less. We give the money and come back."

"Your mother is seriously ill. You haven't seen her in a long time. You should try spending more time with her—and your father. Their situation is precarious."

"They don't need me. They only need the money for treatment."

"That's not true."

"You know nothing about my family. You don't know what my childhood was like. My father is a drunk. He threw me out—"

"Not now," his mother pleaded, drawing his attention to Saaransh.

"So, what? He needs to hear the truth. Your grandfather never cared for anyone in his life. He only lived for himself. He never cared for us, our education—he never even bothered to inquire whether we are alive or dead!" He bristled.

"That was a long time ago. People change. I am sure he has learned his lesson the hard way," his mother replied calmly.

"Not in my family. You know once he threw me out of the house. He wanted me to drop my studies and join his furniture business! I refused. I worked day and night to provide for my education. I slept in the streets. No one came for me. No one even bothered looking for me." He was agitated.

"Just give him a chance," his mother pleaded.

"Not in this life," his father replied resolutely.

"Okay, fine. Just don't create a scene there. Your mother needs you. She is ill. Just remember that."

"I am a self-made man. I have worked hard to provide for everything in life. Nothing has ever come easy for me. I had to work night shifts at a tea stall to save for my school fees. I was a district level champion in school! How many people you know have done what I have achieved?" he gloated.

Saaransh listened to him quietly. There was an awkward silence that ensued. He rolled down the car window. The air smelled foul and rancid. Vacuous expressions greeted wherever he looked. Life seemed stagnant in the town. He was growing uneasy. He wanted to go back.

"I think we are almost there," his mother said, looking out of the window.

His father pulled up the car near an open drain. He got out and with searching eyes began surveying the surroundings.

The house looked like every other house on the street—crumbling and forlorn. There was a chatter of water from sewers that lent sound to the still air. The damp air in the hallway greeted them with casual indifference. Mice nibbled playfully at some edible article down an abandoned washbasin.

The room reeked of medicine and urine. The floor was strewn with discarded tubes and facial tissues. A woman with an inflated body rested peacefully in bed. Her skin was pierced with long surgical needles that drained excess fluid from her body into an oblong sack. She looked pale and sallow.

Saaransh greeted his grandmother with a nervous gesture. She sighed. She then looked at his father and turned her eyes away. His father sat beside her unwillingly.

"How have you been?" he asked. He was disconcerted. She remained quiet.

"*Namaste, maa ji.*" Saaransh's mother greeted his grandmother, embracing her forehead. "You're burning up. Are you taking medicines on time?" she asked worryingly.

"Everything is taken care of. You need not worry." A person responded in grave tone while entering the room. Saaransh touched his grandfather's feet. His father looked away.

"You are here early. You should have informed me before. The lunch isn't ready yet. I have been washing dirty clothes since morning," his grandfather said.

"We left a little early from home since we weren't sure of how long it would take us to reach here. But we picked the shortest route, didn't we?" She looked at his father, hoping to elicit a response. He nodded his head.

"Excuse me. I need some fresh air," his father said, walking out of the room. He narrowly brushed past his father.

Saaransh's grandmother looked at him. A smile appeared at the corner of her lips.

"Look how much you've grown up. The last time I saw you were a toddler. Some rabble-rouser you were," she sighed.

Saaransh grinned.

"You will be fine, grandma." He held her hand warmly.

"I have lived my life," she responded wearily. She closed her eyes and remained quiet for some time.

"Your father is a very stubborn man. He acts tough, but he is soft from inside. A fine, noble man—if there was one. I wish I could have eased some of his pain," she sighed.

"He was a fine sportsman. We had a room full of trophies. He was very specific about their arrangement. He never let us touch them." She smiled.

Saaransh's mother sat patiently, rubbing the soles of his grandmother's feet.

"I wonder...does he ever talk about me?" His grandmother asked.

"Of course, grandma. He loves you. You know...he has been away for so long that he has forgotten what a home is like," he replied.

His grandfather stepped into the room carrying a food tray in his hands.

"Have some fried crispers. They are a specialty here." He poured a spoonful of mint-flavored chutney in two plates and passed them on.

Saaransh squirmed. He wished he could eat somewhere else.

His grandfather looked at him intently. He wanted to say something.

"I want you to come along with me once you're done," he said.

"*Papa ji*, come sit with us," his mother said, making space on the bed.

"No, I am fine," he politely refused.

"Your father was a ruffian." His grandfather grinned, sighing with nostalgia. This was the first time Saaransh had seen him smile. He was a little surprised.

"I always tell people, if your foundation is strong, you can build anything on it. He is a strong man, your father. Stronger than I was."

* * *

Saaransh stepped into a darkened room. His grandfather led the way. There was a musty odor that hung in the air. His grandfather lit a small torch. It shone bright enough to make out objects in the room.

"See this," his grandfather handed him a picture frame. It was a black and white portrait of a man. The camera was uniquely focused on the face. Angular jaws, slightly chubby cheeks, smoky eyes, pompadour hairstyle, slightly parted lips—all the makings of a fashion model.

"Who is this, grandpa?" Saaransh asked.

His grandfather handed him another picture. This one showed a man standing akimbo in front of a movie camera. He looked similar to the man in the previous picture—only slightly older, perhaps. His hair was thrown back by the wind. His face conveyed deep satisfaction. He seemed to look out to the future with promising eyes.

"Grandpa, is this—"

"This is me," his grandfather beamed with pride.

Saaransh was dumbstruck. He looked at his grandfather and compared him with the man in the picture. His grandfather looked old and withered. His fine features were tarnished by age and fatigue. The two men looked nothing similar.

"I was twenty-two when I went to Bombay with the dream of becoming a filmmaker. I became one—except the film flopped. I had put in a lot of money. I was left with nothing. I had to pack my bags and come back."

"Who else knows about this?"

"Our whole family."

"Even dad?"

"Yes. I don't expect him to talk about this—or me—with anyone. He is ashamed."

He took the picture from Saaransh's hand and silently put it back on the shelf where it laid in dark with his other memories.

"I was not wrong. I had my dreams..." He switched off the torchlight.

* * *

His father sat in the verandah with downcast eyes. His mother came and sat beside him. Then Saaransh saw something that he had never witnessed in his life. His father cried. It was simple, effortless. He trembled and kept shaking his head. He murmured something indecipherable to his mother and then embraced her tightly. A truck rolled outside. Its noise drowned the sound of whispers and cries inside.

* * *

That night, back in Chandigarh, Saaransh lay in Akshay's arms—ensconced in his warmth. Their bodies lay covered with sweat. Saaransh saw Akshay's clothes hanging on a washing line. They were bobbling in the breeze. He felt Akshay's hot breath on his skin. It reminded him of how far he had come away from life's regrets—and the nauseating air that housed it all.

Dearest,

While reading Milan Kundera's 'The Unbearable Lightness of Being', I was reminded of a science lecture that I once attended in my early school days. The thought of the sun burning out and getting self-annihilated sometime in the distant future, is one that has terrified many, and for some, it has been one of their earliest brushes with apparent meaninglessness or futility of life. It was also the time when I first learnt about fusion.

The book, set against the backdrop of the Russian invasion of Czechoslovakia in 1968, chronicles and novelizes the everyday life of four people, who play with their own romantic ideals of love and sex, in desperate attempts to achieve freedom from the burden of existence—the utopian lightness of being.

The reason I draw a parallel of nuclear fusion is because Kundera's characters are elemental in nature. Until their paths converge, they exist in isolated spheres of thoughts and ideals, only to be set off into the elemental turbulence of activity, coalition, and gradual decline.

Tomas, a surgeon, philanders from one woman to another, taking great relish in examining their characteristic oddities by using an imaginary scalpel, while retaining his coldness and solitude. For him romantic love and physical love are two irreconcilable desires—the former being his idea of burden, since it entails attachment and responsibility, and latter, his idea of achieving lightness.

Tereza, his wife, follows her romantic pursuits in the form of achieving her husband's loyalty. She is repulsed by the sight of her body and regards it shameful, and grows increasingly burdened and insecure by her husband's need to find intimacy out of their marital union.

Her struggle for lightness is reflected in her acts of humiliation—working as a barmaid, having sex with a stranger, engaging in dissident photojournalism, and defecating in the open.

Franz, who spends his life in rarefied scholarly pursuits, in academia, falls in love with the free-spirited Sabina. He responds to her indifference and strong individualism with amorous display of affection and vows of eternal love. He grows increasingly despondent of being reduced to an intellectual tool-head and wishes to feel the rush of joy and belongingness by participating in protests and struggles, along with the general public.

Sabina, a free-spirited artist, is Franz and Tomas's mistress. She celebrates her rebellion against her puritanical ancestry by painting erotic images and participating in sexual acts with a reckless abandon. She prefers to keep herself intact in her own element, aloof from the teeming multitudes and their collective tastes. Like Tomas, she is stifled by romantic attachments and finds lightness in her repeat acts of betrayal.

"The heaviest of burdens crushes us, we sink beneath it, it pins us to the ground. But in love poetry of every age, the woman longs to be weighed down by the man's body. The heaviest of burdens is therefore simultaneously an image of life's most intense fulfillment. The heavier the burden, the closer our lives come to the earth, the more real and truthful they become. Conversely, the absolute absence of burden causes man to be lighter than air, to soar into heights, take leave of the earth and his earthly being, and become only half real; his movements are as free as they are insignificant. What then shall we choose? Weight or lightness?"

Kundera's work mirrors life. One can picture him with a sly smile and a bemused look on his face, sketching his characters with deep empathy and part mockery. His characters, in their attempts to soar and become lighter than air, become so oppressed by their lightness that they sink quicker than a diving bell. They become victims of their ideals–their own element. But is it possible to drown in your own element?

We read later in the book that Tomas, burdened by his lightness, moves to the countryside with Tereza, in order to make amends with her and lead a solitary lifestyle, filled with simple pleasures. Tereza recognizes her anima and becomes a recluse, finding solace in the company of domestic animals. Sabina, tired by her own betrayals, finds admirers of her art in the USA and settles there permanently. Franz, weary of his intellectual detachment and fear of inviting Sabina's derision, sheds his inhibitions and joins the Grand March, as a protestor playing an active role and seeking comfort in the company of his fellow men.

Life demands surrender. It is said the Sun will burn out in a few billion years from now. The scientists claim that it will lose its life source—the hydrogen fuel—and will annihilate itself. In nuclear fusion, heavier elements are formed from lighter ones. The hydrogen nuclei combine to form a larger nucleus, helium, releasing massive amounts of energy. But what is often overlooked is the fact that for the nuclei to combine, energy is first needed to bring them together, since they carry the same charge. This occurs naturally in stars, through heat and gravitational forces, but it is also possible to do it on earth, between two people who carry the same longing— to combine and perpetuate. They only have to give up resistance. Perhaps then their lightness will no longer be unbearable.

Always,
Me

6

Lightness and Heaviness

Jab koi baat banaaye na bane
Jis ghadi raat chale
Jis ghadi maatami, sunsaan, siyaah raat chale
Paas raho
Mere qaatil, mere dildaar, mere paas raho

"What are you doing up so late?" Akshay asked, entering from the main door. He was carrying a briefcase and an umbrella in his hands. His hair was soaked wet.

"I was waiting for you. You said you would be home early. From where did you get the umbrella?" Saaransh asked, helping him with the briefcase. He had been reading and resting on the couch, listening to Faiz.

"I was caught in the jam. Delhi's traffic is getting worse every day. Makes me regret leaving Chandigarh. Oh, I borrowed that from someone at work. It had started pouring heavily by the time I was about to leave," Akshay replied, handing him the briefcase. He loosened his tie and sat on the couch with his head pushed back, heaving a sigh of relief.

"You've been working late for the last one month. Do they pay you for overtime?" Saaransh asked, clearing his stuff from the couch to make space for Akshay.

"No, I work for same hours. The traffic is getting worse—

I just told you," he replied brusquely. "Could you please turn down that noise? I have heard enough for the day."

"I was listening to Faiz," Saaransh replied. He was hurt. "I thought you liked Faiz."

"I don't have the strength for this," Akshay sighed exasperatedly, burrowing his face between his hands. "What's for dinner?" he asked after a pause.

"Rice and curry. I warmed it just ten minutes ago. I have been waiting for you. I am starved," Saaransh replied, keeping the casserole on the dinner table.

"You should have had dinner then. Why wait when you're hungry?" Akshay replied, taking off his shoes. There were splotches of wet mud on the floor.

Saaransh fumbled for words. "Because...that's what couples do—they have meals together—they wait for each other—and we are a couple." He looked at Akshay, incredulously.

Akshay dismissed his remark nonchalantly. He got up from the couch and took a seat at the dinner table. He gently took the lid off the casserole and poured some rice and gravy on a plate.

"Akshay, is everything alright?" Saaransh asked. He came and sat across the table.

"Uh—what do you mean?" Akshay replied, licking at his fingertips.

"Nothing," Saaransh replied. He kept gazing at Akshay.

"How is your book coming along?" Akshay asked, taking a mouthful from his plate.

"It's coming along rather well—surprisingly. Earlier yesterday I was lamenting about something trivial—a clumsy sentence had been nagging at me. I spent half a day working on it. And at the end, I decided to delete it altogether. The prose read much better afterwards—crisp, rather," Saaransh replied enthusiastically. He felt mildly relieved that Akshay was taking interest in his work.

"Today was the most productive day of the whole month! I finished a chapter, watered the plants, dusted the whole kitchen, and even found time to get the groceries. And imagine who I bumped into—Yusuf!" He went on excitedly.

"Yusuf? What was he doing there?" Akshay asked, taking another mouthful from his plate. He cleaned his right hand with a paper napkin and checked his mobile phone on impulse.

"He had come along with his mother to shop for his new house. He told me Deven would be moving in with him next month. Did Deven talk about it with you?"

"I don't remember. He must have mentioned it. I hardly keep track these days."

"Sounds exciting, right? Deven must be so relieved. I remember how he helped us set up this place when we moved in a year ago. Mom was so upset about the whole idea of us moving in together. I had to fight tooth and nail to convince her! I heard he recently quit his job to work full-time on his new project—some art exhibition."

Akshay nodded his head. He was looking at his mobile screen with keen eyes.

"Anyway, mom and dad are moving here this winter. It will be nice to have someone close live nearby. Delhi can get harsh sometimes. Do you want to have more rice?" Saaransh asked, offering him a clean ladle. He saw that Akshay was about to finish.

"Uh, what? No, I am fine," Akshay replied, looking up briefly.

"How was your day? I forgot to tell you that my work paper on Thumri got published yesterday. I got the call from the person who manages the online portal," Saaransh said, keeping the ladle back on the table.

"Fine."

"Are you still working on the design for the security system?" Saaransh asked. Akshay's noncommittal behavior was increasingly disturbing him.

"Uh-huh."

"You used to be quite excited about it. I read in the newspaper last month that some German company has successfully replicated the complex—"

Akshay burst into laughter. He was busy typing at the keypad, unconcerned.

Saaransh looked at him, aghast. The sound of Akshay's laughter pierced through his chest. He chewed his food slowly, taking longer than usual. He felt a lump tightening in his throat.

"I am sorry. So, you were saying something?" Akshay asked, keeping his phone down and composing himself.

"Akshay, I fe-eel..." Saaransh trembled. His voice conveyed deep anguish. "I feel really lonely," he sighed with resignation. Akshay looked up from his phone with a frown.

"Well, maybe you should get a job then," Akshay said, dismissively.

"You don't think I am working?" Saaransh was deeply offended. He dropped his spoon in shock and disgust.

"A real job—I meant."

"Writing isn't a real job?"

"Look, we both can debate this for hours without reaching any firm conclusion. What do you want me to do?"

"We haven't touched each other in three months. Do you no longer desire me?" Saaransh asked with expectant eyes. He felt a numbing sensation take charge of him. He relaxed his grip on the table and pushed his chair back a little.

Akshay sighed. He swept his hands over his face and leapt

from the table in anger.

"We are working people. Do you have any idea what our life is like?" He swiftly moved to the windows looking out to the balcony and thrust them open.

"We deal with a lot every day. We have to fight hard to maintain our standards." He removed his tie and threw it on the dinner table in a blind rage. He looked at Saaransh with accusing eyes.

"Do you even know how pressurized I am these days at work? The pre-testing results are a nightmare! They will be laying off workers by the end of this year. Do you even know what my life is like? I mean—how selfish you could be! What do you want me to do? Tell me! I certainly don't have the privilege to sit at home and type fancy sentences on a computer!" He spurted in anger.

"Selfish—I?" Saaransh was choked with tears. He got up from the table and looked at Akshay in disbelief.

"I do everything for you, without your asking. Before we had moved in together to this city, I remember you once told me you weren't eating properly at work. You hated the food. I started sending you a lunchbox every day. I never told you it was I who prepared the food. You were ecstatic," Saaransh cried.

"The day you told me you were unable to go for swimming in the morning, I started waking you up early. You never once took my call or texted to tell whether you were up or still sleeping.

The day you told me you weren't able to cope with stress—I, who had never stepped foot in a religious place out of devotion, started going to the temple just to pray for your well-being," Saaransh continued his tirade. Akshay listened silently.

"Every time you asked me to see you, I compromised on my sleep just so that I could manage work and still make time to see you. I did it all willingly—and I never once complained about anything!" Saaransh bellowed. His whole body shook and trembled.

A faint rumble proceeded from the skies outside. Tiny droplets of water started pouring in through the windows. Akshay stepped back and shut the windows tightly. He lit up a cigarette with shaking hands and took a deep puff. He looked unsettled.

"There is never going to be a marriage, Akshay. We will never have kids. We are all we have. Tell me where I am going wrong," Saaransh pleaded.

"I love you, Saaransh. I will never leave you—just remember that," Akshay answered in a solemn tone, turning his face towards Saaransh.

"I know...you have been seeing other men," Saaransh said, wiping his tears. "I know why you come home so late. I cried myself to sleep the first night when it happened. I forgave you, because I thought it would all change once I started confessing my love for you more vocally."

"I love only you. I will always remain emotionally bound to you. I just...just feel so weak sometimes..." Akshay collapsed into tears. He dropped his head and shoulders and leaned on the adjacent wall for support.

"How do you love me? You say you want to spend your life with me—but how? Like this? I will die keeping my promises and waiting for you, but that won't affect you even a trifle. I see this now. You avoid me. You come home late. You refuse to touch me. There are times I feel so lonely here that...that I feel like strangling myself with my bare hands!" Saaransh gasped in horror with widened eyes. His voice echoed around in every corner of the room.

"It was our second anniversary yesterday. You missed it—just like the first time. Why are we even together?"

Akshay looked at him despondently. He staggered

towards Saaransh and gently cupped his hands around Saaransh's face. He looked at him with wistful eyes and replied, "You feel so light...I feel so heavy..."

Dearest,

The idea of our life as a straightforward linear path is delicious but untrue. What happens to the problems that we've had? Are they just in the past? Is it possible that the injuries we sustained as young people stay with us and that we are working through them all the time? In fact, where do we live? And I don't mean what address is on your stationery—where do you live in your mind? Are you working through some earlier injury or trauma? Or are you daydreaming? Or are you thinking about other places altogether? The mind is an incredibly agile, fitful creature, it moves. And I believe that all that we know about the complexity of human psychology, above all, the complexity of neuroses and of problems, and of injuries tells us that it's anything but straight forward. Many of us can spend much of our lives, certainly much of our nightmares, reworking things that have happened earlier.

I have often wondered why people have an overbearing concern to 'bury their past and live in the present'. True, the adage might help in alleviating your distress or assuaging your guilt, as the case maybe, but to ignore that one has had a past is to say that one never existed until the present moment! The present is nothing but the past acting on itself, over and over again. Every new experience you acquire becomes past with the blink of an eye. Yes, you look forward in life but looking forward is not something new. In fact, it's looking forward that you've been doing; it's looking forward that triggers events, which again forces you to look forward. You are a being of present but it is the past that lives. It is the past that factors into your every decision. That's not to say that it chains you but enforces on you a strict sense of identity that one casually throws away into the limbo of other defecated thoughts, and the identity that one finds oneself to be at crossroads with in turning points of life. Add more, multiply less, and above all, accept yourself. That sort of delight in being a part of the glorious history of self, a sweeping tale of fortunes and misfortunes, is the most sincere and human tale that every reader wants to read and every writer wishes to write.

In my most personal moments, I see a scared kid panting hard, struggling to reach the coveted platform at the end of a long staircase. I see people behind him—mocking, belittling and ridiculing his efforts. The kid is convinced that the last step is within his reach, that all his efforts would soon bear fruit, but then the staircases swing back and forth, landing him up in a more debilitating and pressing situation than before. The crowd jeers, the last step waits, and the curtain of life never falls.

Is it I, or that kid that I live?

I have found comfort in your warmth. Your touch has freed me from the tug of memory. No two people could have been happier than we have been; yet there are times I feel I cannot go on for long. There are voices inside my head that I cannot silence. Memory surges, memory acts upon me—the past is not past, it still lives.

Always,
Me

7

Shame

Saaransh sat at the corner of the bed watching the man undress. The man took off his shirt and neatly hung it on the hook. He moved carefully and quietly, at an unhurried pace. He looked at Saaransh and winked.

"Take off your pants," he ordered. Saaransh complied.

The sheets felt cold. Traffic streamed quietly outside the window. The hours of dusk glided past the crowded bylanes. The air was filled with the noise of impatient street hawkers peddling their last wares before closing for the night.

"You are so young...and beautiful...why would a boy like you do this to himself?" the man sighed, moving his hand up Saaransh's thigh and nuzzling at his earlobe. He leaned against Saaransh and pushed him down on the bed.

"My body is dead. My lover doesn't need me," Saaransh replied, staring fixedly at the still ceiling fan. Murk crusted its blunt edges. It hung loosely from the ceiling in utter disrepair and neglect. He felt the man kissing all over his face.

"You are so beautiful...there is nothing like love...we are all bags of shit and blood," the man mumbled.

"He doesn't have time for me. My body disgusts him," Saaransh said.

"Who would deny a beautiful boy like you? Come

closer...I want to taste these fine lips of yours," he said, grabbing Saaransh's chin. Saaransh resisted; the man's touch felt hard and ugly.

"What's the matter? I want to kiss you!" the man retorted in anger.

"No, please, I don't—" The man held him down and planted a forceful kiss.

Saaransh kept his lips sealed. The man pursued vehemently. He tried forcing his tongue inside Saaransh's mouth. He was getting weary and annoyed. He bit at Saaransh's lip in anger. At last, Saaransh relented.

He felt the man's saliva dribbling down his throat. The man moved his wrinkled hands with uncharacteristic firmness. Saaransh grabbed the sheets and crushed them with his fingers. He no longer wanted this. The man bit furiously. Saaransh writhed in pain.

"You should come here often...lucky you came to me...I know how to treat young men like you...I know what you all like..."

A chorus of muffled giggles and chatter rang from outside the room. Saaransh could make out the playful voices of men and women wrapped in intimacy. He convulsed with helplessness.

"Please, let me go," he cried. The man clamped his hand firmly over Saaransh's mouth and pressed in rage. Saaransh gasped for breath. He pleaded the man with his kind eyes. Hot tears streaked his face.

The man lifted Saaransh's legs and forced his way inside him. Saaransh was jolted by the violence. "I promise you'll like it...they all love it...just let it..." he moaned. The man kept tearing through his body, unremittingly.

Saaransh was numbed. He moved his hands across the man's arms and gently fondled him. The man pushed his hands away. He was engrossed in the act. Perspiration ran thick from his forehead.

Saaransh looked at him in wonder. He imagined him to be Akshay. He imagined him oppressing his body; stifling his cries; embracing him lustfully, passionately, in anger, in love, and in pain. He had known love, he thought. He had known touch, he mourned silently.

He prepared himself as the man came. He rolled to one side of the bed as the man gasped and sighed. The man looked satisfied; his thin, ruffled hair betrayed the naked patches on his head. Saaransh gradually put on his clothes.

"We should do this more often," the man said, beaming at Saaransh.

"What's the matter? I thought you liked it," he asked. The man came closer and took Saaransh's hand in his hand. "I really like you. You are so sweet. I want to do everything with you—take you out for coffee, movies, kiss you in the park! I feel lonely here. What's the matter? Why are you shaking?"

Saaransh leapt from the bed in horror and ran to the door. He thundered down the narrow staircase of the hotel. He crashed his elbow against the enclosing wall and bounced outside with a vigorous shove.

Multitudes swarmed before his eyes. He found himself flailing in a sea of people. Onlookers gasped as they cleared the way for him. He ran barefoot; his will lay clutched in his heart. The coarse earth spurned his feet. Sirens and horns roared. Fumes of heat and dust licked at his skin. His whole life flashed across his eyes—fleeting landscapes, moments of warmth, togetherness, laughter, shouts, and cries.

Darkness spewed at him. It soon started to engulf him. He was running at an unrestrained pace. He searched his way through the cobbled streets, fighting the nausea stirring inside him. He soon reached the end of the road and collapsed at the first sight of his residential building.

* * *

"Mom, are you there?" He clutched the receiver with shaking hands, panting heavily.

"Saaransh! What's wrong? Have you been sprinting? You sound out of breath," she answered.

"No...I had gone out for a jog. Just got back some time ago."

"Your father and I were just remembering you. The new tenant is arriving tonight. We are moving all your stuff to the basement. I had no idea you had so many books!"

"How have you been, mom?"

"I am fine. My back still hurts from all the bending that I have been doing for last many days. Your father has other things to look after. There is so much stuff to pack...we are moving out tomorrow."

"I can't wait for you and dad to come to Delhi. I want to see you."

"Is everything alright? You sound tensed."

"Everything's fine, mom. I am just a little tired."

"If it wasn't for your work—and Akshay, I would have never let you leave this city. And now you are not even working! That reminds me—where have you reached with your book?"

"Mom, I need to ask you something."

"Yeah, I am listening. What's wrong? I don't like the way you sound."

"Why do all the people I care about leave me?"

"What are you talking about? I don't understand. Where is Akshay?" she asked, startled.

"Mom, why did Aditya uncle leave us?"

"He was ill, Saaransh. You know that. What has gotten

into you? You are making me worried now."

"When I was young, they said I was ill. And those who saw my illness avoided me. I cried day and night, praying to God to cure my illness. He never listened to me, but Aditya uncle embraced me..."

A stunned silence ensued at his mother's end. He suppressed his tears and continued talking to her.

"He said I was special. He would touch me every day. He taught me how to love...how to kiss. He and I shared everything together. He said he loved me."

His mother let out a silent gasp. She remained still and quiet.

"You say he was ill. I saw him every day. I wonder what his illness was. Aunty and children loved him. They paid him regular visits to the hospital. It was then he started avoiding me. H-He never looked at me the same way...I would drop my pants and kneel down on the floor—just like he would tell me. Still...he left..."

"Saaransh—I—why didn't you tell us?"

"Tell what? That we loved each other? His illness took him away. He was loved even when he was ill...but my illness..." His voice was choked with tears. He held the receiver firmly.

"There is no other room in this world that sees my shame. This room, this bed, it knows me too well now. No one shares it with me anymore. Akshay has left. I wonder...I wonder why I am abandoned..." he sobbed.

"No one has abandoned you. We all love you very much," she replied softly. "Are you listening to me? You are not alone, you were never alone. And you know what your illness is?" she asked, leaning into the receiver.

"My shame..."

"Love. You love too much. There is no closet or room in the world that can hide your love."

"But I have lost on love. It is too strong…it will never touch me again…"

"Love will find you. You know why? Earlier today I was cleaning your room when I found an old poster rolled behind a pile of books. Do you know what poster I am talking about?"

"No…"

"It is the one with Byron's quote written on it: Love will find a way through paths where wolves fear to prey. You remember now? You must have bought it when you were twelve or eleven years old. You were too young to understand it then, and I don't think you still do."

He sighed. He remembered it faintly.

"You are golden, Saaransh, always remember that. Love will come knocking at your doorstep when you least expect it to."

Dearest,

By the time you will have received this letter, I would be gone far away.

You've been gone for three days now. No one knows where you are. Your phone has remained switched off for all this while. Mom said you would be back soon. She and dad are taking good care of me.

The electricity came late in the morning. I had been rolling in the bed all night, with one arm wound tightly under my abdomen, to relieve the pain that had been gnawing at me for the last many months but got unbearable only last night. In that moment, while I lay crouched in bed, sweating through the sheets, came a realization: there is no comfort in death; and it can come anytime, to anyone. I tried taking my mind off it, focusing on the greater sufferings in the world, of people who die every minute, of terminal illness, in war, accidents, genocides, natural disasters; some who find the courage to take the bullet directly to the head, while others who are slowly devoured by time or disease; but nothing would ease the malady that had been plaguing my heart.

I have been a self-contained, rather a lonely person all through my life, and I have only tried to avoid the uncomfortable knowledge by filling my hours with achievements, mainly academic, in the hope that someday the desperate years I spend toiling contain the meaning and soundness to escape the mundaneness of everyday life and the shame attached to my past. I am terrified of high-rise buildings, crowded stations, streets bustling with activity, anything that pushes me in the background, stands high above me, and uses my insecurities to threaten me. No wonder I've loved the limelight and attention.

When you came in my life, I thought I needed nothing

else. You made me feel loved, desired, and respected. With you, I could let my guard down for a while and just melt in your warmth. My body started responding to me in ways that I had never thought. For the first time, I silently acknowledged how frustrated and lonely I had been and how I only needed one touch in the right place to untie the knots in my body. You have not been faithful, and I still try to make my peace with it.

I know life is getting steadily tougher for you. I understand that I can't demand your time like I used to before. I take myself out on lonely dates, invoking your presence in my mind, to lend me the gratification that I yearn for. It has been nearly nine months and we haven't touched each other. I don't think about it too much, but if you were in my place, would you have been equally patient and understanding? You and I know both know the answer to that. I know it's wrong to force one's definition of love on the other. No one should bear the burden of the other's love.

Last night, I saw my whole life ahead of me: passing from body to body, in the vain hope of finding love, by making false promises of togetherness amidst juxtaposing loyalties, and getting crippled by the anxiety of finding nothing but a spiritless void, a terrible longing for romance, a longing for that fleeting happiness that love provides; and since happiness is nothing but a longing for repetition, people's lives move in circles. I had a friend once who thought she had found love, and fearing that a moment so pure and unreal would never come again, claimed her life by jumping off of a rooftop. When I saw the picture of her body, lying in a pool of blood, I remembered her smile, and I tried searching for it in her scarred face. I couldn't find it. And I look at myself; I fear the same.

Fearing this madness would grip me sooner or later, I purchased a ring two days ago. I haven't worn it yet. I want to wear it now. There is no one I want to be with more than you; but I know we can't be together, no matter how hard I try, I will suffer from nothing but the longing itself.

I am leaving this city. I don't know when I will be back. I don't think I can stay here any longer.

Always,
Me

Keepers and Guardians

"Siddharth, I forgot to tell you, someone came looking for you three days ago, referring to an essay that you once wrote for your research—something related to Indian Classical music. Do you have any idea what he was talking about?" Radhika asked.

How could anyone know that? Siddharth wondered. It had been years since someone mentioned his essay. He was pleasantly surprised.

"Did he leave a name?" he asked.

"Yes—Gautam Kaul. He said he wanted to contact you. I refused to provide him any information, at first—but he was very insistent. I gave him your old e-mail address—the one that you were using back in Chandigarh. I told him you had been gone for years and preferred to retain your privacy."

"And? What did he say?"

"He said he respected that. He just wanted to write to you. Did you get any e-mail recently?"

"I don't even remember my password. It has been ages since I logged on to my old e-mail account. I will have to see. This is odd. I mean—I don't even recall anyone by that name."

"Whatever you say, he seemed pretty determined to contact you. Read whatever he has sent and tell me later."

"Okay. Just let me get my laptop, first. I will call you back. Bye."

Siddharth was greatly relieved when he succeeded in logging on to the server on his third attempt. There were more than a thousand unread e-mails from his friends and distant relatives. He searched for the person's name and found his e-mail at the top. He quickly opened it and began reading.

* * *

The rain poured down in torrents from the sky. An earthy fragrance pervaded the air. The sky had acquired an inky sheen since early afternoon. Little streams of water gurgled in the narrow conduits along the mountain slopes. People rushed to find shelter under the erected tarpaulins.

Siddharth reached the end of the road and stood to scrutinize the signboard that pointed to the Tiger Eye Resort. The rain poured swiftly. He followed the directions into a village. The path was matted with bits of wet thatch and animal fodder. He reached the guesthouse after half a mile trek.

Siddharth found Phil in the waiting cabin near the reception, getting ready to leave. He was wearing gumboots and firmly held a mackintosh under his arm. He seemed anxiously waiting for something.

"Phil?" Siddharth called to him.

"Hey, man! What brings you here?" Phil asked, surprised. He came forward and shook hands with Siddharth.

"Phil, I can see that you are getting late. May I have a word with you? I won't take more than five minutes. I promise," Siddharth said.

"Yeah, tell me. I was waiting for my cab. It is on its way. Is everything alright?" Phil asked, moving towards a couch.

"Yes, everything is fine. I just wanted to give you something," Siddharth replied, taking a seat on the couch.

"Me? What?" He was startled.

Siddharth fished out a small cardboard box from his jacket and handed it over to Phil.

"Open it," Siddharth said.

Phil opened the box and found a shiny silver ring encased within it. There was a tiny slip of folded paper under the ring.

"But I don't understand," Phil asked, perplexed.

"I purchased this ring when I was twenty-five. I used all my savings and even sold some of my belongings to get the money. This ring has kept me alive for ten years. It is a promise I made with myself. I have honored that promise every day of my life. I want you to have it now," Siddharth said.

"But I can't—it is your wedding ring!" Phil protested.

"Phil, this is not a gift. That slip of paper has my address. Pay to me whenever you have the money," Siddharth replied calmly.

"But still—"

"You are smart, bold, and courageous, Phil. But do you know what your problem is? You think you have time." Phil went silent.

"Love is rare, Phil. Millions are perishing every day in strange places—for the lack of it. No one knows them; their suffering goes unaccounted. They assume different identities, live in distant lands, bury themselves under hard regimens—but love continues to elude them." Phil listened quietly.

"I want you to go and marry that girl, Phil. Now. Do I make myself clear?" Siddharth asked, sternly.

"Yes, sir," Phil replied, brushing away a rolling tear. He was overcome with gratitude. The rain pelted at the cabin windows. The evening was drawing near.

"But where do you go from here?" Phil asked innocently.

"I am leaving tonight for my village in Shimla. I have a new lesson plan to work on from tomorrow. It is a busy year ahead. We will be starting with the annual day rehearsals soon," Siddharth replied.

"How may I help you?" Phil asked.

Siddharth smiled at him. He sensed Phil's eagerness to repay him for the gesture.

"Send me a postcard from Missouri. I will be waiting for that."

Dear Gautam,

This e-mail came to me as a special one. Who wouldn't be flattered with those kind words of yours? I can imagine it might not have been easy for you to write that e-mail to me, as is the case for me to reply in a manner that might not in any way be misconstrued.

Today is my last day in Manali. I wish I could capture every scent and sight and take it all along wherever I go. This has been a tremendously absorbing travel experience. I came here alone, seeking answers to questions that have bothered me for some time. The experience has been nothing short of liberating.

There was a running theme in almost all the conversations I had with people here: Loneliness. Teenage life can be dauntingly lonesome. The pressure to fit in, stand out, or stay neutral, can bring out the worst in some people. Those who try seeking validation from an authoritative figure might find themselves to be largely misunderstood. Meanwhile, adults, after having acquired sufficient degree of freedom and propriety, find themselves obsessing over the lack of meaning—or getting order—in their lives. Some try filling the void through companionship; others through work; and some, both.

An adult is no stranger to the lonesome life of a teenager, but after seeing the hard face of life, his idealism is numbed and he is embarrassed to identify with his former self. People with families might have to deal with children who grow up resenting them; partners who walk out on them; or worse, loss of a loved one. The grief can be shattering. For years, there may be no consolation in sight. The truth is, while teenage life can be frustratingly lonesome, nothing prepares one for lonesomeness of adult life. It's when one recognizes loneliness as a condition and not an enforced discipline or punishment, one learns true humility. Practicing small acts of kindness and compassion in everyday life can go a long way in helping endure the lonesomeness of adult life and restoring faith in humanity.

I have struggled all my life understanding romantic relationships. I feel most romantic relationships end, not because two people can't make it work anymore, but most of the time we keep pining over the initial thrill and excitement that falling in love provides; and when after a while things grow less intense and become increasingly quiescent, the heart, forever raging with a lust for unknown pleasures, rebels. People keep falling in and out of love all the time. Those who stick together know that loving can be hard.

Sex can be a great glue when two people start off together. To embrace the body of the lover, in its nakedness, its flaws and perfection, is one of the great joys of falling in love and being with your lover. The intensity would dampen with time, but this is where the learning begins. Once you know about each other's weaknesses and strengths, and have been exposed to your own vulnerable side, lovemaking is tenderer, gentler, and probably more routine. It will lack the thrill of discovery and excitement, but for those who wait and survive the period of confusion and frustration, it can be a rewarding experience—for learning is a life-long process and love will peak when you least expect it to.

There is no end to finding a better person. The world is a concrete jungle; you will always find people who are better than your lover, in some way or the other. It is not about a finding a better person; it is about making it better with the one you truly love. You will fall in love with yourself over a thousand times, if you make that happen.

Gautam, I am a man dedicated to my lover and have the greatest fortune of having immense love in return—something I wish to every person in this world. At thirty-five, your e-mail may be the sole inspiration for me to write my first book. You are extremely articulate and clear at a rather young age. And trust me your life is just about to begin in many ways. And I have a feeling it would be full of wonderful stuff.

You can reach me anytime on this e-mail address. Stay connected. I hope to meet you someday, soon.

Warmly,
Siddharth

THE END

BEST READER AWARD

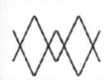

Name of the book:_____

Name:_____

Address:_____

_____

_____

Age:_____ Mobile no._____ Occupation:_____

Email:_____

CONTEST GUIDELINES

*Readers are required to write a review on the book and post them on Amazon, Goodreads and Facebook.
*Fill in this form, scan it and email us along with your review at **bestreaderaward@wovenwordspublishers.net**
*The email subject line should be "Your Name-Name of the title reviewed."
*This is an annual contest. Awards will be declared on our website www.wovenwordspublishers.net

To send the submission through post, please send it to:
**Woven Words Publishers, Vill: Raipur, P.O: Raipur Paschimbar, Dist: Purba Midnapore, Pin: 721401, West Bengal, India
Mobile: +917501586381**

© Woven Words Publishers OPC Pvt. Ltd.

SHORT STORY AND POETRY CONTEST

Name:_____

Address:_____

_____

_____

Age:_____ Mobile no._____ Occupation:_____

Email:_____

Title of the story/poetry:_____

CONTEST GUIDELINES

*One submission per candidate.
*Short stories up to 1000 words and poem of not more than 45 lines.
*Fill in this form, scan it and email us along with your story/poetry at **contest@wovenwordspublishers.net**
*The email subject line should be "Your Name-Name of the submission."
*This is an annual contest.
*Awards will be declared on our website www.wovenwordspublishers.net

To send the submission through post, please send it to:
**Woven Words Publishers, Vill: Raipur, P.O: Raipur Paschimbar, Dist: Purba Midnapore, Pin: 721401, West Bengal, India
Mobile: +917501586381**

© Woven Words Publishers OPC Pvt. Ltd.

Manufactured by Amazon.ca
Acheson, AB